ALL I COULD NEVER BE

ALL I COULD NEVER BE

A NOVEL

ANZIA YEZIERSKA

INTRODUCTION BY
Catherine Rottenberg

A Karen and Michael Braziller Book
PERSEA BOOKS / NEW YORK

All I Could Never Be was originally published in 1932
by Brewer, Warren & Putnam, New York.
First published in a new edition by Persea Books in 2020.

The Publisher gratefully acknowledges The Feinstein Center,
Temple University, whose generous grant helped make publication of thi
new edition possible, and Alice Kessler-Harris, for her insight, expertise, and
guidance in publishing the work of Anzia Yezierska from 1975 until now.

Requests for permission should be addressed to the publisher:

Persea Books
90 Broad Street
New York, NY 10004

or sent via email to permissions@perseabooks.com.
For more information, consult our web site: www.perseabooks.com.

Library of Congress Cataloging-in-Publication Data

Names: Yezierska, Anzia, 1880?–1970 author.
Title: All I could never be : a novel / Anzia Yezierska ;
introduction by Catherine Rottenberg.
Description: New York : Persea Books, [2016] | „1932 |
"A Karen and Michael Braziller Book."
Identifiers: LCCN 2016003730 | ISBN 9780892554652 (pbk. : alk. paper)
Subjects: LCSH: Jewish fiction.
Classification: LCC PS3547.E95 A79 2016 | DDC 813/.54—dc23
LC record available at http://lccn.loc.gov/2016003730

Design and composition by Rita Lascaro
Manufactured in the United States of America

First printing, 2020

To my daughter, Louise

INTRODUCTION

Catherine Rottenberg

Anzia Yezierska's literary texts have generated increasing scholarly interest over the past few decades. This is true not only within Jewish American studies, where students are very often required to read her work, but also more broadly within immigrant, women's, and multi-ethnic studies. Yezierska's best known novel, *Bread Givers* (1925) is now considered a modern classic—at least in the Jewish American literary tradition—and has become a cornerstone in numerous university and college courses. Yet, like so many women novelists of previous centuries, Yezierska's canonical status is a phenomenon of the recent past. Although the young Eastern European Jewish immigrant experienced a "meteoritic rise" to fame in the early 1920s (Stubbs ix), which catapulted her into the literary limelight and briefly to Hollywood, her popularity was short-lived in her own lifetime. Already by the Depression Era—a mere ten years after the publication of her well-received short stories—Yezierska's gritty depictions of poor Jewish immigrants on the Lower East Side had fallen out of favor. It would take approximately forty years of obscurity and the feminist momentum of the 1970s before Yezierska and her works were rediscovered.

When *Bread Givers* was first reissued in 1975 by Persea Books, Alice Kessler-Harris noted in her introduction that few people had, at the time, even heard of the once-famous writer Anzia Yezierska. In the years that followed, however, Kessler-Harris's pioneering research on the forgotten "sweatshop Cinderella" as well as her determination to republish Yezierska's fiction would significantly change this cultural amnesia. The timing was right; there was a receptive audience for Yezierska's vivid narratives about independent-minded, working-class immigrant women. *Bread Givers* succeeded in a big way, welcomed by both the general reader and educators, and is still widely read. In addition, three collections of Yezierska's short stories (*Hungry Hearts, The Open Cage,* and *How I Found America*) as well as two other novels have been successfully reprinted: *Salome of the Tenements* in 1995 and *Arrogant Beggar* in 1996. Today, it is no longer unusual to see one of her two (still) lesser known novels appear on university syllabi or reading-group lists, and there is currently a small but growing cadre of dedicated Yezierska scholars. Thus, in the second decade of the twenty-first century, Kessler-Harris's early statement has become happily anachronistic.

Since the 1980s, and similar to other minority literatures in the United States, many previously "lost" Jewish American texts have been rediscovered. Yet, it seems fair to say that few if any early twentieth-century Jewish American authors have elicited the amount or the kind of interest that Yezierska has. Unlike contemporaneous authors, such as Samuel Ornitz, Ludwig

Lewisohn, or Sydney Nyburg, Yezierska's fiction has appealed to a much wider and more diverse audience. This appeal has to do, in large part, with the forceful way her fiction continuously returns to a theme that still resonates strongly in the United States: the dilemma of being strong-willed, female, ambitious, and part of a minority group whose cultural norms and traditions clash with the dominant culture.

YEZIERSKA'S LIFE

In her 1995 introduction to *Salome of the Tenements*, Gay Wilentz perceptively describes Yezierska as the author of semi-fictional autobiography and semi-auto-biographical fiction (x). It could easily be claimed, for instance, that Yezierska often created her protagonists very much in her own image. By all accounts—and analogous to her fictional women characters—Yezierska had an extraordinary driving will and an intense, explosive, and impassioned personality (Gornick viii). However, due to Yezierska's tendency to "mythologize" her own personal history, it has taken scholars many years to sift fact from fiction as they have attempted to piece together an accurate portrayal of the author's life.

Today we know that Anzia Yezierska was born in the Russian-Polish village of Plostk sometime in the early 1880s. Her mother, father, three brothers, and three sisters (two more brothers were born after the family's emigration) arrived at Castle Garden around 1890; she was between eight and ten years old. And like so many Jewish immigrants who arrived from Eastern Europe during these years, the family settled in the already vastly overcrowded Lower East Side. Anzia's father was a Hebrew scholar who continued to devote his time to religious study in the New World; this meant that the other members were responsible for supporting the family economically. Too young to work in the sweatshops, Anzia was initially sent to the public school. Her formal schooling did not last long, though, and she was soon forced to quit school and enter the workforce in various low-paid jobs: as a servant, a scrub woman, a laundress, and a factory worker. But ever eager to learn, Anzia diligently attended night school, even after working ten-hour shifts.

In her late teens, Anzia moved into the Clara de Hirsch Home for working girls in order to escape her family with whom she was constantly at odds. She soon chafed under the rigidity of the settlement house as well, for she was not one who could live long according the dictates of others. Anzia was, as her daughter Louise would later describe her, "a rebel against every established order" (Henriksen 6). Yet Anzia was also apparently armed with an impressive ability to persuade people to do her bidding, and she eventually convinced a few of the wealthy patrons of the settlement house to cover her tuition so that she could attend Columbia University. In 1904, after four years of study, Anzia earned a degree in domestic science from Columbia University Teacher's College and subsequently worked intermittently as a teacher.

But Anzia did not take to teaching either, particularly the teaching of domestic science, and she toyed with the idea of acting, briefly attending the American

Academy of Dramatic Arts on scholarship. During this period she also tried living at the socialist Rand School, and, in 1910, when already in her late twenties, experimented with matrimony. Her first marriage lasted less than a year, and her second marriage took place soon after the annulment of the first. As Katherine Stubbs recounts, Anzia chose to have a religious ceremony the second time around so that the marriage would not be legally binding (ix). Before separating from her second husband, Anzia gave birth to her daughter, Louise Levitas, in 1912. Louise was, however, to spend most of her childhood years living with her father and grandmother.

In her biography of her mother, Louise reconstructs these years of indecision—between married life and being single and between different career options— narrating how Anzia found inspiration in and from her older sister, Annie, who told vivid stories about her life of poverty in the Lower East Side ghetto. Louise suggests that it was "Annie's mimicking of her children and neighbors" (21) that first motivated her mother to write short stories. Disillusioned with teaching and estranged from her second husband, Anzia decided to become a writer.

It was also during this period that Anzia first met John Dewey, the well-known and respected professor of philosophy at Columbia University. This encounter in 1917, when Anzia was around thirty-seven years old, would change the course of her life. Anzia initially approached Dewey—bursting into his office unannounced, as the legend goes—in order to ask for help in gaining a better teaching position. Given her larger-than-life personality, it seems that Anzia's determination, passion, and unconventionality captivated Dewey, so much so that he eventually presented her with her first typewriter and introduced her short stories to magazine editors whom he knew. He also encouraged her to audit his graduate seminar in social and political philosophy. As the relationship developed, Dewey ensured that Anzia was hired as a translator for a research project—very like the one described in *All I Could Never Be*—whose goal was to investigate the Polish community in Philadelphia. The wages were generous enough to enable Anzia to spend most of her time writing. However, this project also proved to be the beginning of the end of Anzia's relationship with Dewey, whose short-lived passion for this Eastern European woman has been immortalized in the poetry he wrote to her.[1] While the real-life relationship ended abruptly, likely as a result of Yezierska's refusing Dewey's sexual overtures, Dewey had already left a profound and lasting mark on Anzia and on her writing. Many scholars have noted that Dewey-like figures constantly appear in various guises throughout Anzia's fiction.

Perhaps ironically, it was only after this intense relationship fell apart that Anzia's career as a writer finally took off. Her first story had been published in 1915, and from 1915–1919 there was a steady trickle of stories, one of which—"The Fat of the Land"—was chosen by editor Edward J. O'Brian as the best short story of 1919.[2] Less than a year later, Houghton Mifflin published a collection of her stories under the title *Hungry Hearts*. Success bred success at this stage; her stories sold, and not long afterward, the Hollywood producer Samuel Goldwyn paid her ten thousand dollars for the film rights to her book. And so Anzia left for Hollywood; she was close to forty years old.

But Anzia, being Anzia, was also unable to accommodate herself to Hollywood. Katherine Stubbs writes that the fierce commercialism of the motion picture industry shocked her and she objected to the way Goldwyn Pictures altered her novel's plot for commercial considerations (x). By all accounts, Anzia developed writer's block and felt stifled by the frantic competition and the whirlwind race toward the spotlight (Stubbs xii). She returned to New York and continued to write. But the times were changing.

Anzia published four more books in the next decade: *Salome of the Tenements* (1922, which was also made into a movie); the short-story collection *Children of Loneliness* (1923), *Bread Givers* (1925), and *Arrogant Beggar* (1927). While *Salome* met with mixed reviews, *Bread Givers* was admired "as a colorful, suspenseful narrative of family tensions in the ghetto." The positive reviews of her second novel revived Anzia's reputation for a short time, but when her third novel appeared in 1927, the reviews were not only lukewarm but were also few and far between. The sales of her fourth novel, *All I Could Never Be*, published during the Depression years, were paltry. As her daughter tells it: "The fad for Anzia Yezierska had apparently passed" (Henriksen 2). Thus, by the late 1920s Anzia's literary fame had already ebbed.

Eighteen years of "silence" followed—years in which Anzia continued writing but could not get published. In the interim she worked various jobs, among them a job on the New Deal's Works Progress Administration Writers Project. She produced and published one final full-length text, *Red Ribbon on a White Horse,* in 1950. Although she received the best reviews of her career for this semi-fictional autobiography, the book "died at birth" (Henriksen 3). From the 1950s until her death in 1970, Yezierska never stopped writing: she wrote review essays for the *New York Times Book Review* and short stories about old age.

Anzia Yezierska died in relative obscurity. She did not live to see the latest revival of her literary fame— a revival that, unlike the previous ones, appears set to last.

THE WORK: *ALL I COULD NEVER BE*

Given the broad consensus regarding Yezierska's canonical place in Jewish American Studies and the growing consensus regarding her established place within American letters more generally, it was quite surprising to me when I first discovered that the last of her four surviving novels, *All I Could Never Be,* had been out of print for decades.[3] I was acquainted with the basic outline of the plot—as a result of reading the few scholarly articles that discuss the book—but I had never read the entire novel. Following my decision to obtain a copy, I found that the novel was unavailable in most of the hundreds of university libraries in the United States. Not even the famed Butler Library at

Yezierska's alma mater, Columbia University, housed
a copy. Thus, when I finally managed to find the novel,
I read it with great anticipation.

I was not disappointed. All of those elements that
make Yezierska's novels particularly Yezierskian
are there: the unique mix of melodrama, sentimental
romance, and realism; the relatively loose form and plot
structure, the grittiness and peculiar pace of her prose;
and, finally, the obsessive theme that drives so many of
her narratives—the desire of the immigrant female protagonist to "make herself for a person" (*BG* 66).

All I Could Never Be tells the story of a vibrant and
talented Jewish woman, Fanya Ivanowna. Raised in
dire poverty in Poland, Fanya eventually finds her
way to America, where she is convinced she can create her own—better—future. She lives and works on
the Jewish Lower East Side, toiling away but desperate for companionship and understanding. Trying to
"better herself" but completely alone in the world,
she attends events offered by the settlement houses in
the neighborhood. She is electrified by one of the lec-
tures she hears, which is given by a well-known educa-
tor Henry Scott, the most transparent of all Yezierska's
fictionalized John Deweys. This lecture changes the
course of her life, since Fanya is impetuous and strong-
willed enough to seek out Scott in his university office
and ask him to read an autobiography she has written.
This leads to a highly charged exchange between the
scientifically-minded and rational, older Anglo-Saxon
and the passionate and young Jewish immigrant. Scott
is immediately impressed by Fanya and offers her a

job as a translator with a group of sociologists studying Polish immigrant life in the United States. Despite her best efforts, however, Fanya can never quite fit into this group of intellectual observers, and the novel ascribes this failure to Fanya's insistence on the affective rather than the rational aspect of life.

A little later in the narrative, Scott, who is married, makes sexual advances to his young protégé; although Fanya loves him, she is confused and rejects these advances. This, then, marks the end of their intimate relationship. Yet, Fanya's experiences with Scott are portrayed as precipitating her decision to become a writer. For years afterward, Fanya imagines herself still in love with Scott, and following her success as an author she even attempts to rekindle the relationship. This attempt fails miserably, and, once again, Fanya decides to start her life anew, this time by leaving the Lower East Side and New York City behind her. She buys a house in a small New England town, where, eventually, a painter-turned-hobo comes into her life. This non-Jewish but fellow immigrant (from Russian Poland) ignites Fanya's passion, and the reader is made to understand that Fanya has finally found peace as well as created a home for herself in America.

There are, of course, many aspects of the narrative that are reminiscent of Yezierska's earlier works. Fanya is yet another one of Yezierska's indomitable female characters. Moreover, Fanya's story, like the stories of Sara Smolinsky, Adele Lindner, and Sonya Vrunsky before her, is one that underscores the potential payoff of perseverance, independence, and hard work on the one hand, and the profound loneliness and alienation of being an immigrant and female rebel on the other. Fanya, yet again like all Yezierska's protagonists in her full-length fiction, manages—against tremendous odds—to realize her talent, and eventually even finds a "true" soulmate after the disastrous false start with Henry Scott. Indeed, Fanya's overall trajectory is almost identical to that of Yezierska's other unforgettable female characters: they all manage to fulfill themselves professionally or artistically and ultimately find like-minded men who complement and encourage their life decisions as well as their ambitions.

In the rare cases where contemporary critics do discuss Yezierska's fourth novel in any detail, they most often focus on the relationship between Fanya and Henry Scott, which they rightly claim is the story of Anzia's relationship with John Dewey, "thinly disguised as fiction." They also note that *All I Could Never Be* is the most autobiographical of Yezierska's novels (see, for example, Dayton-Wood 216). While I am indebted to the work of earlier scholars, I would like to turn critical attention to the way in which *All I Could Never Be* actually diverges quite significantly from Yezierska's previous full-length fiction. This divergence, I propose, revolves primarily around the text's portrayal of "Jewishness." Whereas in her earlier novels, the female protagonists ultimately end up working and living side-by-side with their Jewish partners (on the Lower East Side), this later novel presents us with a female protagonist who, in the end,

is not poised to marry a Jewish soulmate but to con-
summate a union with a *non-Jewish* immigrant in a
small New England town.

This, I believe, is a striking difference and one
well worth dwelling upon. If Yezierska's writing has,
in many ways, come to stand in for or represent early
twentieth-century Jewish-American fiction, then it
seems particularly important to investigate her changing depictions of Jewishness and Jewish otherness.
Yezierska's early fiction, and most particularly her
first novel, *Salome of the Tenements*, clearly and unam-
biguously articulates Jewish difference in racialized
terms. The Jewish protagonist Sonya Vrunsky's marriage to the Anglo-Saxon millionaire philanthropist
John Manning is described not in terms of interfaith
matrimony but in terms of racial mixing and miscege-
nation.[4] Yet, by the time *All I Could Never Be* is written,
Yezierska seems to have incorporated more fully the
notion of nation into the conversation about Jewish
(and other "ethnic") difference.

This is not serendipitous. Scholars of Jewish history, such as Deborah Dash Moore and Hasia Diner,
have already detailed just how transformative the
inter-war years were for the Jewish community in the
United States. Diner, for instance, has underscored
that although Jews' entry and eventual acceptance
into mainstream society was a lengthy and complicated process, the years 1924-1948—during which
Jewish immigration from Eastern Europe all but
came to halt—were pivotal for transmuting the Jewish
American community from an immigrant one to one in

which the American-born out-numbered those of foreign birth (Diner 240). Kessler-Harris has suggested
that the 1920s and 1930s were particularly challenging
for the Jewish community. Precisely at a time when
Jews had begun entering the institutions of higher
education and a range of middle-class professions in
expanding numbers, local community networks began
to break down as a result of the Great Depression. This
meant that as the Jewish community made noticeable
inroads into the middle class during these years, Jews
themselves became less dependent on the resources
of their neighborhood and more dependent on those
of the municipality, the state, and federal govern-
ment.[5] All of these factors clearly contributed to the
way in which Jews were being positioned with respect
to American institutions as well as the way in which
Jews themselves—Jews like Anzia Yezierska—perceived their own position vis-à-vis dominant white
Anglo-Saxon culture.

In the biography of her mother, Louise recounts
how Yezierska initially had ended *All I Could Never Be*
with the protagonist's return to the Lower East Side.
The biography even includes a fragment from the original conclusion, which reads: "Bathed in the poetry of
ancestral memories, it seemed to [Fanya] there was
only one way to go on—to go back to her roots—back to
the ghetto" (quoted in Henriksen: 242). It was the publisher, George Palmer Putman, who apparently helped
convince Yezierska that this ending was both unsat-
isfactory and unbelievable. From Louise's account,
at least, it does not seem that much persuasion was

necessary.[6] The two-chapter epilogue that Yezierska eventually wrote and the one that now concludes the novel, then, must be understood not only in terms of what Yezierska herself could—by the Depression-era—envision as an alternative and possible ending to Fanya's search for a home, but also gestures to a profound shift in the way Jewishness was being imagined in the culture more generally.

Scholars such as Karen Brodkin (1998), Eric Goldstein (2001), and Matthew Jacobson (1998) have convincingly argued that although "Jewishness" as an identity category was still framed within a discourse of race during the Jazz Age and throughout the 1930s, it was to undergo a radical sea change as the century progressed: namely, Jewishness was slowly morphed from a racial category into something that would later be articulated as white ethnicity. *All I Could Never Be*, I believe, can be understood to both reflect and to participate in this process of disarticulating "Jewishness" from a racial discourse. The particular ending with which Yezierska ultimately decided to conclude her novel, as well as her publisher's pressure on her, both gesture toward the shifting and, consequently, unstable signification of Jewishness during these years.

Indeed, in sharp contrast to *Salome of the Tenements*, in which intermarriage is offered only to be dismissed as an impossibility (due to irreconcilable racial differences between Jew and Gentile), in *All I Could Never Be*, the partnership between Jewish and Gentile immigrants in small-town America is held up as not only possible but as perhaps the only bridge to a more integrated and accepting society. Though the text intimates that the cultural gulf between native Anglo-Saxon and immigrant Jew (read Henry Scott and Fanya) may still be too wide, barring any possibility of intimate union *at least for the moment*, the affinity between the Russian-Polish immigrants (Fanya and her painter-turned-hobo) ultimately trumps the ostensible Jewish-Gentile divide. Nationality rather than "racial" similarity takes precedence, complicating the notion of Jewishness as a distinct racial category.

Jewish racial otherness is thus no longer taken for granted in *All I Could Never Be*, or at least does not signify in the same way as it did in Yezierska's earlier fiction. The novel's detailed depiction of Dewey-cum-Scott and his concept of cultural pluralism and internationalism—where America becomes the meeting ground of "all the nations of the world," blazing a trail of "internationalism for other countries to follow" (31)— facilitates Yezierska's ability to self-consciously meditate on what constitutes "Jewishness." The novel's fixation on Scott, in other words, makes the alternative and current ending perfectly compatible with the narrative trajectory, and, consequently quite "believable." Thus, in contrast to Louise's claim in her biography that the epilogue was merely tacked on, I suggest that the conclusion well suits the novel's (likely unwitting) inchoate disaggregation of Jewishness from its racial tether.

The novel does not, of course, ultimately provide any clear cut answers to these meditations on

Jewishness. Rather, the text raises the question of Jewish difference throughout the narrative only to displace it in the end by raising the specter of "something deeper, more far-reaching than the race barrier" (*AICNB* 188). This elusive something materializes in Oakdale, the small New England town where Fanya finally settles. This "something" that is deeper than race is never defined, but appears to be related in some way to class status and more specifically to *downward* mobility. While Fanya, the now middle-class Jewish immigrant, has been accepted into the New England town, there are other "others" who are ostracized and rejected by the respectable inhabitants of Oakdale. The despised "other" in the town is not the Jew, it turns out, but rather the previously upper middle-class woman, Jane, who had once belonged to the wealthiest and best family in town (*AICNB* 183) but who has since—due her family's bad investments and financial ruin—spiraled down the class ladder into abject poverty. It is almost as if the novel positions the determined and active Jewish immigrant as the one (best) able to fulfill the promise of the American Dream while contrasting her to the once privileged "native aristocrat of Oakdale" (*AICNB* 196) who has passively accepted her bad fortune. As a result, the narrative ultimately deflects attention away from the question of Jewish otherness by positing a more profound difference than the (Jewish) race barrier. If intermarriage between Jew and Gentile can become desirable, and if Jewishness is no longer irreconcilable with quintessential small town American life, then Jewish difference—whether conceived in racial or national terms—no longer seems to make much difference at all. And this, it is important to remember, is a far cry from Yezierska's other novels in which Jewishness and the Jewish space of the Lower East Side still play a determining role in the protagonists' decisions up until the very final moments of the narratives.

Meredith Goldsmith has pointed out that unlike Yezierska's other novels, in which the Jewish Lower East Side is still posited as a potential place where Jews can negotiate if not merge upward mobility with a supportive community, *All I Could Never Be* offers the American small town as a positive and alternative space for its female protagonist.[7] Building on this insight, I suggest that Yezierska's Depression novel may offer the New England town as potentially better suited to fashioning a new mode of Jewish *Americanness*. Indeed, it may be that her 1930s novel, which depicts the moving out of the Lower East Side, presages and, as I suggest above, participates in the morphing of Jewishness into a white ethnic identity—a process that would only be complete in the post-Second World War era.

At the same time, and paradoxically, it might also be the recalibration and increasing acceptance of Jewish difference that *All I Could Never Be* dramatizes that can help account for why Yezierska and her work lost cultural currency during the 1930s. Not unlike the novel's protagonist, by the mid-decades of the twentieth century, many Jewish Americans had moved out

of their "ethnic" ghetto; they were no longer interested in the ghetto they had just left and were not
yet ready to be reminded of their quite recent entry
into the middle-class. Gaining fame for her portrayal
of the teeming, dirty, and poverty-ridden Lower East
Side, Yezierska could not then symbolize Jewish-
Americanness again until Jews in the United States
had become fully accepted white (middle-class) nor-
mative Americans and were able to look back nostal-
gically at the Lower East Side from a place of security.[8]

Today—at a time when many Jewish Americans
(as well as other white ethnic minorities) are con-
cerned with maintaining a sense of uniqueness and
ethnic particularity—Yezierska's early fiction (with its
strong Jewish female protagonists eventually discov-
ering their Jewish soulmates and making good on the
Lower East Side) suits a contemporary and collective
yearning. Seen from this perspective, it is not surprising that *Bread Givers* has been lovingly embraced. On
the other hand, her final surviving novel, *All I Could
Never Be*, which celebrates intermarriage and where
a shared national origin trumps or even elides Jewish
particularity, is likely to be more disconcerting for a
contemporary audience. After all, Jewish organiza-
tions have for some time been loudly lamenting the
fact that approximately half of all Jewish Americans
are currently marrying non-Jews. Yet, it is precisely
this unsettling potential—both in terms of how scholars have understood Yezierska's oeuvre as well as the
themes it raises, such as the generative potential of
intermarriage—that makes the republication of this

novel at this particular historical juncture so important. Indeed, *All I Could Never Be* may presage yet
another transmutation of Jewish American identity in
and for the twenty-first century.

C.R., 2020

CATHERINE ROTTENBERG is a native New Yorker. She earned
her B.A. in Jewish Studies at Brown University, and her M.A.
and Ph.D. in English Literature at the Hebrew University of
Jerusalem. From 2008 to 2016, Dr. Rottenberg was on the faculty
of Ben-Gurion University of the Negev. Presently, she teaches
American Studies at the University of Nottingham. She is the
author of *The Rise of Neoliberal Feminism* (Oxford University
Press, 2018) and one of the authors of *The Care Manifesto* (Verso
Books, 2020), among other publications.

NOTES

1 In *Anzia Yezierska: A Writer's Life*, Louise Levitas Henriksen,
Anzia's daughter, tells the story of how the poems were discovered in the Columbia professor's wastebasket and rescued
by one of Dewey's students. Scholars did not know to whom
these passionate poems were written until Jo Ann Boyston, a
Dewey expert, stumbled upon two of these very same poems
(though slightly edited) in Yezierska's novels.

2 Edward J. O'Brian was the well-respected editor of *The Best
Short Stories* series, which (after the first edition) was published by Small, Maynard & Company until 1926.

3 According to Alice Kessler-Harris, Yezierska wrote and
destroyed two unfinished manuscripts after the publication
of *All I Could Never Be* (*BG* xi).

4 Here I am thinking particularly of the scene in which the protagonist Sonya Vrunsky, the Russian Jewish immigrant, and
John Manning, the Anglo-Saxon millionaire, hold a marriage
reception at Manning's mansion. Manning's "people" refer to
Sonya in racial terms and describe her as lacking breeding,
culture, and tradition; namely a "mere creature of sex" and a
"pet monkey" (*ST* 127–8). See my *Performing Americanness*.

5 Alice Kessler-Harris discussed these issues with me in a
personal correspondence. See also Deborah Dash Moore, *At*

Home in America: Second Generation New York Jews; and Hasia
Diner, *The Jews of the United States*, pp 205–259.
6   Henriksen, pp. 242–243.
7   Goldsmith makes this point in an unpublished manuscript.
    See, for example, Hasia Diner's *Lower East Side Memories*.

BIBLIOGRAPHY

WORKS BY ANZIA YEZIERSKA

All I Could Never Be. 1932. New York: Persea Books, 2020.
Arrogant Beggar. 1927. Durham, Duke University Press, 1996.
Bread Givers. 1925. New York: Persea Books, 1975, 2003.
How I Found America: Collected Stories of Anzia Yezierska. New
    York, Persea Books, 1991.
Hungry Hearts and Other Stories. 1920. New York, Persea Books,
    1985.
The Open Cage: An Anzia Yezierska Collection. Ed. Alice Kessler-
    Harris. New York, Persea Books, 1979.
Red Ribbon on a White Horse. 1950. New York: Persea Books, 1981.
Salome of the Tenements. 1923: Urbana: University of Illinois
    Press, 1995.

OTHER SOURCES

Brodkin, Karen. *How Jews Became White Folks and What That Says
    About Race in America*. New Brunswick: Rutgers University
    Press, 1998.
Dash Moore, Deborah. *At Home in America: Second Generation
    New York Jews*. New York: Columbia University Press, 1981.
Dayton-Wood, Amy. "What College Has Done for Me: Anzia
    Yezierska and the Problem of Progressive Education." *College
    English*. Vol. 74, no. 3 (2012), 215–233.
Diner, Hasia. *The Jews of the United States: 1654 to 2000*. Berkeley:
    University of California Press, 2004.
Diner, Hasia. *Lower East Side Memories: A Jewish Place in America*.
    Princeton: Princeton University Press, 2000.
Goldstein, Eric. "The Unstable Other: Locating the Jew in
    Progressive-Era American Racial Discourse." *American
    Jewish History* 89, no. 4 (2001): 383–409.
Henriksen, Louise Levitas. *Anzia Yezierska: A Writer's Life*. New
    Brunswick: Rutgers University Press, 1988.
Jacobson, Matthew. *Whiteness of a Different Color*. Cambridge, MA:
    Harvard University Press, 1998.

Mikkelsen, Ann. "From Sympathy to Empathy: Anzia Yezierska and the Transformation of the American Subject." *American Literature* Vol. 82, no. 2 (2010), 361–388.

Gornick, Vivian. "Introduction." *Hungry Hearts.*

Kessler-Harris, Alice. "Introduction." *Bread Givers.*

Kessler-Harris, Alice. "Introduction." *The Open Cage.*

Rottenberg, Catherine. *Black Harlem and the Jewish Lower East Side: Narratives Out of Time.* Albany, NY: SUNY Press, 2013.

Rottenberg, Catherine. *Performing Americanness: Race, Class and Gender in Modern African-American and Jewish-American Literature.* Lebanon, NH: University Press of New England, 2008.

Stubbs, Katherine. "Introduction." *Arrogant Beggar.*

Wilentz, Gay. "Introduction." *Salome of the Tenements.*

ALL I COULD NEVER BE

All I could never be,
All, men ignored in me,
This, I was worth to God, whose wheel the pitcher shaped.

—From "Rabbi Ben Ezra," by Robert Browning

When Fanya was seven years old, her mother tied a little bag about her neck, the beggar's bag. She was sending her to their rich cousin in Warsaw to beg for the family.

"Tell them if they don't help us we're lost," said her mother, pushing the beggar's bag down her shirt. "Tell them since Father died we have no one but them to look to for bread. The roof is leaking and the window is broken, and to all our black luck, the cow stopped giving milk."

Fanya was too thrilled with the prospect of going to her rich cousins to hear her mother's droning voice of worry. Every day was a holiday at her cousin's. Each meal a feast of plenty. White bread and meat for dinner and wonderful fruit and cake. Last winter when her mother had sent her with the beggar's bag on her neck, her cousin had not only put in ten rubles, but also allowed her to stay for two days. Two days of heaven. And the things they gave her! A warm shirt and a brown dress with gold buttons. A coat with a fur collar almost as good as new, and a red ribbon for her braids. Ribbon for her hair the first time in her life.

"Mother! Please—*please*—let me wear my Sabbath dress," Fanya pleaded, so excited with the vision of her cousin's house that she had forgotten her mother's refusal only a moment before.

"God on earth! How that child tortures me! Didn't I tell you ten times already—no—*No!*"

"Why not?"

"Bandit! Stop eating out my heart."

"But mother, this is all holes."

"A fire should burn you! The waters should drown you! A Sabbath dress wills itself in you! What? What is your great joy? Why so happy with yourself? The stove is broken, the roof leaks, the cow stopped giving milk—I'm sending you to beg a few rubles and you want to make it a holiday?"

"But what harm is it if I wear the Sabbath . . . "

"Oi-oi-oi! From tar and from pitch you can tear yourself away, but when she begins a thing—"

"Then tell me, why not?"

"Witch! What do you want from my life? Do I have to tell you why not? Show yourself to them with a decent dress—and back you come without a ruble!"

Fanya bit her lip with a trembling between retort and tears. She darted a look of rage at the stony gloom in her mother's face, then sullenly jerked on her grease-spotted rag of a dress.

One last attempt to make herself presentable. She picked up the broken mirror from the shelf, to fix her hair. While her mother was busy preparing her lunch, Fanya stealthily snatched the red ribbon from the trunk and tied her hair with it in defiance of her mother and the pack of worries that had turned her into a scolding hag.

A student from the house nearby came with pen and ink to write the name and address of her cousin in Warsaw, on a piece of white muslin. This her mother sewed on her dress.

"How can you send a child so far away, alone?" asked a neighbor.

"What? You want me to go? They'd give me good advice how to be economical. But when they see a child, they take their hand away from their heart and do something."

Her mother, once started, launched forth in a storm of abuse against the "stingy rich," and kept it up all the way to the station.

"If they had any fear of God, doesn't it say it's their duty to help the poor widows and orphans? Why should they have everything and us nothing? For them, satin furniture and velvet curtains—and for us, the worst hut in the village that nobody else would put their foot in."

Fanya found shelter from her mother's tirade, dreaming her dreams. She saw herself in her cousin's house, seated, like a queen, in the black satin chair, while tea was being served. Perhaps there would be a ride on the merry-go-round. And, even a treat at the confectioner's shop.

As the coach came in sight, a sudden fear darkened the child's eyes. At her cousin's they were so very clean, they made her wash and wash again before they let her sit down with them at the table.

"Look! Is it clean behind my ears?" she asked anxiously.

"It's too clean yet, for the way I feel," shrilled the nerve-racked mother. "My bitter heart on them for being so crazy clean. What else have they to do but wash themselves all day long? I could also be a lady, if I could sit back in an easy chair with nothing to do, nothing to worry about, while the servants brought me the eating to the hand."

A new world opened for Fanya looking out of the stagecoach window. The broad, spacious fields that rolled by blotted out the straw-thatched huts where the families were huddled together with the hens and the little chicks in one dingy room. In scrappy patches of ground bordering the huts crowded the cabbages and potatoes.

Nearer and nearer came the town with the grand houses of brick and stone, tiled roofs and many windows. And best of all, the fenced lawns full of gleaming flowers. The cabbage patches of her village had no need for fences. And poor people had no time to play with flowers.

Once at her cousin's, Fanya forgot the black luck story her mother had dinned into her ears, about the broken stove, the leaking roof, and the cow stopping to give milk. As before, her clean cousin again found fault with her cleanliness. Again she suffered the embarrassment of being sent to the washroom to scrub face and neck and ears. But later, at dinner, her plate was filled again and again. They watched enviously the ravenous appetite that none of their wealth could buy.

As in her dreams, after dinner, they let her sit in the black satin chair. "What beautiful hair!" said her cousin, admiringly, loosening Fanya's braids and spreading them out like a halo of curling gold about her head.

Suddenly, a look of unutterable disgust came into her cousin's eyes. "Oh-oh-oh-oh!" she sprang away in recoil. Fanya saw her motion to her husband and whisper something. One shuddering word—"*Lice!*"—plunged like a knife through the child's helpless body.

"Come!—No—Go in the garden and wait," came in a horrified voice from her cousin.

They did not let her come into the house again. Cast out—a pariah from whom even the stable boy shrank.

Presently her cousin returned. With aloof, shivering fingers, she thrust money into the beggar's bag. Then a servant hurried the condemned child to the station, walking at arm's length all the way.

Fanya remained tensely silent. Lips drawn into a tight line. Eyes grimly staring ahead. The little face was drained of all color. The features rigidly set, hard as stone. Not a whimper escaped her. But inside the coach, out of sight of her outraged relatives and the scornful servant, the tension broke. Hiding herself in a corner—alone—apart, moans of grief burst from the depths of her shame.

A startled conductor and passengers tried to comfort her. Kind hands, kind voices reached out to her. They offered candy and fruit, but Fanya only shuddered at their kindness and motioned them away.

"Oi-i-weh! Turned you back with nothing?" cried her mother, as Fanya stumbled into the house, sobbing. She snatched at the bag. Fear fled from her eyes as she felt the gold coins.

"Why—fifteen rubles! Then why your tears?"

"They—they—"

"What is it? Tell me!" Her mother jerked her roughly.

"They—they—" A world of woe crowded into her throat at the wretched ending of her dreams.

"But fifteen rubles!" her mother marveled. For a while at least, there would be respite from the fight with the grocer and butcher. And she rushed out, too elated with the sudden relief from worry and want to think again of the child's distress.

Her mother had long since died, but the beggar's bag, which she had tied about Fanya's neck at seven, was still upon her at seventeen.

Bargain Day. The air was loud with the clamor of bargain-hunters. Greedy eyes darted here and there and everywhere—drunk with the desire to possess everything they saw. To Fanya's distracted gaze, floor-walkers, cash-girls, saleswomen and the grabbing crowds of shoppers whirled about in crazy circles.

Shrill voices, a sea of grasping hands were tearing at her to wait on them all at the same time.

"Here! Hurry! I'm next!... Say!... Wait on me. I've got to get home.... Give me those stockings in tens.... I want a lighter shade. No, this is too light.... This is too dark.... See here! These are marked wrong.... Hey! I came ahead of her.... Miss! There's a thread loose in that heel...."

Into this bedlam of confusion came a quiet voice:

"Please let me have a pair of two-dollar gun-metal stockings, size eight."

Fanya, bending over the counter, and conscious only of a confusion of faces and voices, looked up quickly: she knew that voice.

A pair of cool blue eyes, sympathetic and humorous, looked into hers.

Miss Farnsworth was tall, slender, and blonde, with an out-of-doors appearance which added to her charm. She was club-leader of Fanya's club, and had helped Fanya get this jwya was grateful. And there was no one she would rather have seen at this moment with all this unaccustomed noise and violence beating on her.

"A hectic day, isn't it?" she said, handing Fanya a bill. "It must be pretty trying, I expect..."

"*Trying!*" She would have liked to add, "You're the only customer today who knew what she wanted." But she had learned that a department store is all ears—for those who say the wrong thing. So she smiled instead—as cheerfully as she could.

"Well, you'll have a holiday tomorrow—Thanksgiving—"

"No holiday for me."

"How's that?"

"Thanksgiving and Christmas are the loneliest days of the year for me. Makes me think of people with homes."

Miss Farnsworth was curious to know more of the girl behind the counter.

"You have no home?"

"Would you call a hall-room a home?"

"Are you really alone?" Miss Farnsworth was even

more interested. "Would you care to have Thanksgiving dinner with us? Just mother and me. It wouldn't be a bit exciting, but I'd love you to come."

"What? Thanksgiving dinner with you? You mean it?"

"Please come," said Miss Farnsworth, writing down her address and handing it to Fanya with a cordial smile. Then she was gone, and took a kindly world with her: people closed in on Fanya again, faces and questions and complaints.

*　*　*

Sutton Place. The very name of the street had distinction. No crowds. No tenements. Every house was different. You could see and feel—even from the outside—homes were inside of them.

She stopped in front of a Dutch colonial house with graveled paths, blue spruce and gay window boxes running over with ivy and golden bittersweet. Music came from the open window. A duet, piano and violin. Music—not the raucous shrillness of a worn-out phonograph. Songs that she never could sing, thoughts that she never could voice, suddenly grew clear. Lines from an old reader fused with the rhythm of the melody, voicing her sentimental mood:

> "From the soul of man who was homeless,
>   Came the deathless cry of home;
>   And the praises of rest are chanted best
>   By those who are forced to roam."

Only after the playing ceased did Fanya remember to ring the bell. The maid who opened the door looked like a figure in an old painting. Someone who had grown up with the home and become a part of the home—not a hired servant.

"I'm so glad to see you," Miss Farnsworth greeted her. Her mother rose from the piano to add her welcome.

"It's kind of you to come."

"It was wonderful of you to ask me."

"Take off your wraps in the guest room," said Miss Farnsworth, leading her through the hall.

Guest room! She was too excited to note anything distinctly except the blue and gold of the furnishings and the view overlooking a rock garden. A rock garden in New York City!

"I heard you as I came up. Will you play the same piece again?"

"Yes, after dinner. It's the cook's afternoon off and we want her to have as much of it as possible."

Even considerate of their cook! No wonder the maid who opened the door had such a friendly smile. To be a servant in this house—what a chance for friendship and love.

The spirit of the house seemed to manifest itself best in the air of simplicity that pervaded the dining room. The fine, old, white linen, the shimmering silver and glass—nothing escaped Fanya's gaze; but the roses in the center of the table went to her head like wine. As they sat down, she leaned forward to inhale them greedily.

"How I love the smell of them! The color and the perfume of these roses—why think of dinner!"

"Why not have both?" laughed Miss Farnsworth,

amused and a little taken aback by such an unre-
strained show of emotion.

"Both?" Her mother's poverty-crushed look came
into Fanya's eyes. The fear and worry dinned into her
ears from infancy came into the quaver of her voice.
"Both—here on earth? That couldn't be. I'd die of too
much..."

"The world is full of roses and dinners—enough for
everyone." This came with such quiet composure from
Mrs. Farnsworth, Fanya did not venture to disagree.
In the freeing atmosphere of these "superior" people,
she felt all sense of poverty and limitation must vanish
from her soul.

And then the dinner was served. Fruit cocktails—
made from fresh, ripe fruit. Vegetable soup—rich with
the color and aroma of the garden—turkey, cranberry
sauce, and deep-dish apple-pie. Such delectable food,
served as they served it, was food turned to poetry
and music.

A delicious content stole over Fanya as they rose
from the table and seated themselves in the living
room.

"What would you like to have us play for you, my
dear?"

"Oh, anything. What was that piece I heard when I
came in? I don't know a thing about music, but I love
it so."

"That was a sonata by Cesar Franck. Isn't it sad he
never knew how great his music was? He died in poverty, before his genius was recognized."

They who shine in the light—how they sympathize

with those who die in the dark! Who'd believe the rich could be so human? How it had been drummed into her ears about the "bloody rich," the "heartless rich"! Poorest people couldn't be more warm-hearted, more giving of themselves.

Fanya looked from Miss Farnsworth's buoyant youth to the smiling face of her mother. Serenity, fulfillment enhanced the glow of the white-haired face. No drawn lines of pain, disease or worry, no slumping of the figure, no weary eyes as with the mothers of the poor.

The harmony within them was in all the things that surrounded them. Beauty was in that house, but not the kind to be bought in shops. Beauty that had grown and ripened from generation to generation. Her hand ran over the arm of her chair to feel the texture of the old fabric. The rug on the floor, the portraits on the wall, the whatnot with quaint family keepsakes—colors and lines of everything in the room seemed to blend into one another.

Fanya had always thought of art as something apart from life, to be seen at exhibitions, kept safe in a museum. Here art was the breath of their lives. It was in the thoughts they thought, the love they felt, the way they served their dinner, the treatment of their servants, the warm welcome that greeted the stranger in their home.

Later in the afternoon, Miss Farnsworth opened an old mahogany cabinet and brought forth curios, rare embroideries, carvings in ivory and jade.

"These are some of the things Great-grandfather

brought home when he was in the China trade, a hundred years ago," explained Miss Farnsworth.

Fanya touched them with appreciative fingers. "They are very, very beautiful," she said.

"Would you like to have a little memento of our Thanksgiving dinner?" asked the mother. "This fan—or this Buddha?"

"Oh, you've already given me so much."

The afternoon was over too soon.

"We'll see you again, won't we?" said Mrs. Farnsworth, as Fanya rose to go.

"Whenever you'll invite me. I don't get such invitations every day of my life."

"I'm going to have some friends for tea next Sunday. Perhaps you can come then? I'll write you before the week's up."

Fanya was at the door and Mrs. Farnsworth called her back. "Won't you take these with you?" she said, offering the roses.

Fanya opened her mouth to speak, but no words came to her lips.

Roses for her! The intoxicating beauty of them seemed to stab awake every sorrow she had known.

Back in her room, she placed the flowers in a milk bottle on the trunk that served as her table and dresser. Behind the roses, Fanya kept seeing the beautiful madonna face, the white hair, the kind eyes. Love seemed to shine from their serene depths. The music, the hospitality and above all, the gracious gift of the roses—she had to write out all it had meant to her.

"Madonna! Mother-spirit!
Beautiful One of the snow-white hair—friend of the
    red roses!
Let me warm my lost, homeless heart on your breast.
I'm so cold, so starved, so maddened with loneliness,
All my life I've been choking with tears;
Always driven back upon myself.
No one wanted the love I burned to give.
Cast out—homeless—in a city of a million homes.
Oh, Beautiful One of the snow-white hair—friend of
    the red roses!
Take me in your arms and kiss me, and hold me close;
And in your loving warmth, close against your breast,
    let flow my tears."

Without stopping to read what she had written, Fanya sent to her newfound friend the effusive sentimentality of her seventeen years.

The release of sharing with a kindred heart what she felt. She went about smiling, visualizing to herself the emotion in Mrs. Farnsworth's face as she read each line, and then read it again to Edith. She saw mother and daughter turn their gaze away to hide the rush of sympathy filling their eyes. She herself almost wept, as she saw in fancy the flaming words of their response.

How eagerly she waited for their answer. She questioned the janitor, watched for the postman to make sure it would not go astray.

But days passed. Weeks. And there was no letter, no answer to hers. Not even the promised invitation.

A bewildered sense of shame and confusion stunned

her. What was it she had done? Why—how—had she lost them?

Slowly the bitterness of being ignored seeped through her flesh. She had humbled herself, exposed the famine of her soul to strangers. In her loneliness—her social famine—she had mistaken a little friendliness, a gesture of politeness, for personal response.

And she never went to the club again for fear of meeting Miss Farnsworth.

PART I

CHAPTER I

Crowded into the settlement house auditorium was a conglomerate gathering of many nationalities. Thoughtful faces, young, eager faces, grey, worn, wrinkled faces that were as eager. Clean-shaven clerks, pushcart peddlers, tailors, gaunt factory girls—all sublimating their thwarted social life in intellectual interests. Misfits in the social scheme trying to find where they belonged, following every free lecture on music, painting, poetry, philosophy, or sociology with the same indiscriminate ardor with which their elders followed the exhortations of their rabbis. People in their ignorance worshipping the god of knowledge.

Fanya had come earlier than usual that night, and, pushing in at the head of the crowd, had managed to get herself a good seat near the front.

"I'm in luck tonight," she thought. "It was worthwhile not stopping to eat supper."

She settled herself comfortably, and her thoughts drifted away on the gathering tide of human voices. She came back to earth with a start. The noise around had suddenly subsided into whispers and coughs and the grating of chair legs. A little door opened at the end of the hall, and Henry Scott walked in. Like a man who is undertaking a somewhat distasteful job, he walked hurriedly to his table, laid his books on it, played with them nervously for a moment or two, and then looked up at his audience.

Fanya had watched it many times before—this reluctant, unconvincing entrance, and then the way in which everything would be changed the moment he looked at them.

His noble head and fine grey eyes contrasted strangely with a slipshod appearance—clothes worn anyhow, pockets bulging with papers, tie crooked, often as not a boot-lace hanging. He looked like a small-town lawyer or tradesman, but Fanya's fanatic idealism made him the symbol of all she could never be. He was free of their sordid bondage for bread. He was culture, leisure, the freedom and glamour of the "Higher Life."

He looked at them in silence, half smiling, while the whispers and the laughter, last echoes of interrupted conversations died away before him.

"The most primitive form of society presents to us a picture of continuous strife," he began. "The quarrel-some caveman feared and hated every other caveman who was not of his tribe. The hand of each member of one tribe was raised against each member of all other tribes. Savage man and his kindred considered it noble to kill the stranger."

There flashed before Fanya the red-faced police-man, gesticulating with his club, as he led an old push-cart peddler to the station house for selling bananas without a license.

"Stick to your Hester Street. Chelsea section belongs to the Irish."

"Among the Greeks," Scott went on, "the word 'stranger' or 'foreigner' was the same word as 'enemy.' The Greek code of morality was to be kind and hospitable and generous to those they knew and ruthless to everyone else."

His face lighted into a broad smile.

"We have the same example of closed societies in the insect world. The ants of one hill recognize one another by the scent of the hill and attack every strange ant in sight. And there are the pariah dogs of Oriental towns. The dogs of one street will not tolerate a dog from another street and the strange dog is in danger of his life."

The eyes of his East Side audience, growing wide with his words, like children listening to a fairy tale, flashed to Scott an opposite picture—the wandering, vapid gaze of the college students who took his courses to bite off required credits. He loved these people. Their hunger—the vitality they exuded—brought him a fresh realization of what he was trying to tell them.

His glance, moving from one side of the room to the other, fell on Fanya's vivid face, and stayed there a long moment. The unconscious flattery of her eyes— more than that, her whole stored up vitality—caught him and lured him from his habitual abstraction. For the rest of the evening he was half aware that what he was saying was directed to her—half aware of a pale face, and burning eyes, and red hair, putting themselves between his thoughts and his words . . .

"In England, as late as Thackeray, the Scotch were so hated that a Scotch girl had to have lots of money

before a well-bred English family would accept her
as a daughter-in-law, just as is the case with the
American girl in France today. The prejudice against
the Irish also in England was so strong that advertisements for workers of any kind often ended with 'NO
IRISH NEED APPLY.'"

His words blew away the walls around Fanya and
led her out of the stifling narrowness of her life to the
wide sunlit shores of universal experience.

"The globe grows smaller and smaller. The radio,
the airship, the wireless, mass production necessi-
tating foreign markets are breaking down the barrier between nations and races, making of the whole
universe one community. People today know more of
what is happening in China than they used to know of
what was happening in the next village. We have been
forced out of our national boundaries into racial units.
And now we are slowly beginning to struggle out of
our racial antipathies to realize that there's no more
reason to hate another race than there was for savage
man to hate members of another tribe."

He fumbled in his pocket as he spoke and drew out
a crumpled handkerchief and a much crushed, folded
envelope, on the back of which he had summed up his
points. The gesture made Fanya smile. She noticed
the loose shoelace dangling from his old-fashioned
high shoes, and his tie knotted awkwardly to one side.
He was a man too absorbed in his work to look at a
mirror, she decided. His simplicity made his great-
ness less formidable. He was like Moses, Isaiah, who
lifted the multitude to the heights by the force of their

prophecies. Her swift imagination went on creating him in the image of her own desire as she listened.

"America, the meeting ground of all the nations of the world, must blaze a trail of internationalism for other countries to follow. Not in flaunting her strength as a giant, but bending in helpfulness over a sick and wounded world, like a Good Samaritan. Not in pride, arrogance, and disdain of other races and peoples, but in sympathy, love, and understanding."

How far removed was the vision he projected from the life she had lived! One corner of her mind listened intently while the rest of her went on formulating the imaginary questions she would ask him.

In his low monotone, he summed up his talk:

"Every time you accept with dignity and philosophy some discrimination that is part of the old black past lingering into the present, you are chipping off another flake from the great rock of misunderstanding that bars the way for all—for *all*, I repeat, not merely those discriminated against. For there is a growing realization of the solidarity of the human race—that what hurts and diminishes one hurts and diminishes all in the end.

"When you have learned to look at your relations with other races in a broad, impersonal way, you have laid another stone on the road to the future where human beings will no longer be taken as members of a group for which they are not responsible but as individuals on their own merits."

After the lecture, on her way out of the crowded auditorium, Fanya bumped against Zelda, the pockmarked old maid who worked with her in the shirt factory. Zelda had spent her youth preparing to enter a college that barred her on account of her age and race. Breathless fervor now animated her starved face. She had suddenly grown taller and straighter. Henry Scott had given her a place in history. Her problems were world problems. She was part of an historic process of emancipation of mankind from prejudice and ignorance.

CHAPTER II

F anya hesitated at the door of his office. Even though she had spoken to him before, his remoteness made him still unreal. She still experienced an awful stage fright, a dazzling self-consciousness.

Leaning against the door in her confusion, she saw herself in the mirror that hung at the end of the hall. Red hair. A tense, white face—without powder, without rouge. A startling face above the plain, dark, un-modish clothes.

With quick determination, she pressed the button. The door opened and Henry Scott stood there. He seemed to fill the air with his quiet power.

"Come in, Miss Ivanowna," he invited. The calm quiet of that voice. The kindness of it.

She looked at him in blind hero-worship. The fine, noble head, the white hair like warm sunlight about his face, the kindness that looked out of his grey eyes— even the way his hands rested in his pockets etched themselves indelibly upon her mind.

As she followed him into the room, she caught his quick inquiring glance and the droll twist of his eyebrows.

He pulled out a chair, and, turning away from his crowded desk, sat down beside her. The leisured way in which he leaned back put her at her ease.

Her voice was as resolute as her eyes:

"Isn't it strange—my coming to you—from the other end of the world? Each one is so driven by his own work. How is it you're not too busy to listen to me?"

"One sometimes entertains angels unawares," he smiled.

"Angels unawares!" The Biblical phrase reminded her of her father, whose conversation was always colored with words from the Bible. For an instant, Henry Scott had a strange resemblance to him. Her feeling of familiarity shocked and amazed her. Absurd! Her father had lived and died in the ghetto of Poland. This man, a Gentile—an American. And yet, for all their difference, there was that unworldly look about Henry Scott's eyes that made her feel her father. Her father as he might have been in a new world.

"What I had to say to you was so clear in my mind. And now it's all gone."

A faint smile came over his face, but it only increased her embarrassment.

"If it's important, it will come back to you," he said with his leisured calm. Watching his serenity, she folded her hands quietly in her lap.

"They say the really great people always have time. It's only the little people that are in such a nervous rush. Just the same, if I hadn't something important, I wouldn't have dared to interrupt you like this—"

"This interruption is just what I needed." He tilted back his chair with contented ease. "I've been sitting here for days, scanning bulletins and books on statistics. I was growing stale. Even the trees on the campus seemed withered with my own fatigue—"

Fanya looked up. He—fatigued—stale? The smiling repose of the infinite was in his face.

"As a matter of fact," he went on, in his low monotone, "I've been shut up here for nearly a fortnight to lay out a plan of investigation which has to be ready by tomorrow—"

"It's a study of the Polish immigrant—isn't it?" she broke in. "I read about it in the papers. It said in that interview that you were going to direct it. That's what made me come to you."

She thrust into his hands her manuscript, crumpled from endless rounds through the mail. "I thought maybe my story would interest you. All my twenty-three years are in these pages."

He read the first few lines.

"That's just the thing I want"—he said, his low voice rising to enthusiasm, "just what we need—personal histories."

His eyes searched her face with new interest. He seemed to catch glimpses of her far-off alien ancestry.

"How will you set about to know the Poles?" she asked. "How can Americans with their cold hearts and clear heads ever come to know people burning up with a million volatile ideas?"

His eyebrows raised slightly but he made no answer. He just looked at her quietly, alive to the challenge in her query.

"I hope it won't be another study of the poor," she said. "Words. Grand words, but nothing back of them."

"Why do you say that?"

"Didn't you say in the paper that America was coming to be a meeting ground of all the peoples of the earth?" Her voice took on a sharp, shrill note of doubt. "I wonder—Where do we meet? How do we meet?"

He leaned toward her from his chair, holding her still with the steady gaze of his grey-blue eyes.

"Our whole history is one of assimilation. We began as Anglo-Saxons. And look at our country now! Jews, Italians, Poles—all the nations of the world are weaving themselves into this interracial symphony."

Deep lines knotted her forehead. There rose before her the thwarted, inarticulate, starved lives she knew in the factory. Crowded blocks of Poles, Jews, Italians, who had lost their own national heritage and had not gained a true American one. Islands of foreign-born, who remained shut out of America, shut out from one another, behind the barrier of their racial differences.

"Symphony of nations!" she reiterated his words in emphatic denial. "If you knew the rumble of discord, the jarring and clashing of nationalities that really goes on! Who cares for the culture immigrants bring with them? They may sell the labor of their bodies. But how many get the chance to give to America the hopes in their hearts, the dreams of their minds?"

"What about Michael Pupin, Edward Bok, Steinmetz?"

"What about the countless millions who remain hands for the machines? Fodder for mills and mines?"

"For those who are ambitious, there are free night-schools," he countered, calmly.

"Yes. Night-schools—after a long day's toil. We foreigners are the orphans, the stepchildren of America. The old world is dead behind us, and the new world—about which we dreamed and about which you lectured to us—is not yet born."

He leaned back, looking at the ceiling, deeply thoughtful. Then he turned his gaze back at her as though seeing through her and beyond her.

"It's too bad that there should be this sense of barrier," he observed. "Certainly Americans are not conscious of causing it. Isn't it possible that the barriers you feel are to some extent in your own mind?"

"What do you mean?"

"Those barriers would cease to exist if you could be made to see that they do not exist. There's a story of a man who thought he heard a wolf scraping at his door. Terror gripped his heart and he died."

He paused, waiting for her to speak, but she was examining the old bitter grudge from the new perspective he opened. The whole picture of the way the immigrant built up a barrier of imagined insult and injury against America rose before her eyes. Jews lived in fear of persecution they had suffered in times past. And Gentiles resented what past persecution had made of Jews. She remembered the time when as a child she was turned out of her aunt's house because she was dirty. Ever since then, she had lived in fear of clean people. Cleanliness had come to mean to her heartlessness. And yet she knew there must be clean people in this world who were also human.

"It's the fear in us that kills us," she said, thinking

aloud. "No wonder they say the fear of losing a job is worse than being without a job."

He turned to her with a look that made her aware of something special and rare in herself.

"I wonder whether I am as ready to learn from you as you are from me?"

She laughed freely, gaily. He made her feel that she knew more than she thought she knew.

"What have I to teach you? I have so much to learn."

He smiled down at her. Fanya marveled at the sudden release that filled the moment so completely—she could be so still. It was as though Henry Scott had touched her with his quieting hands and breathed over her his calm.

There was a sense of wide, unshadowed brightness about her as he shook hands at the door. Twice he had unbound her from the prison of her thoughts—by letting her talk, and by talking to her in his silence.

CHAPTER III

The morning after her first meeting with Scott, though she had gone to work in the factory and sat with the same girls at the same machines, there had been a transforming holiday spirit about her, and in her eyes the excitement of a shop full of workers out on a Sunday picnic. The drab buttons she stitched had gleamed like pearls through her fingers.

On her way back from work, people had turned to gaze at her naked bliss. Jostled and pushed by the subway mob, she had thought of so much she wanted to write to him, but in her room, when she put pencil to paper, she could only wrest out of herself one line—a line without beginning and without end.

"Generations of stifled words—reaching out to you—aching for utterance—dying on my lips unuttered—"

She did not sign it.

She put it in an envelope and addressed it to him; she hoped he would know who had written it; she hoped perhaps he might answer; but she did not care very much—it was something she *had* to write to him, and that was all there was to it.

* * *

(But he did know. It lay on the middle of his blotter,

a violently large pencil scrawl on a torn piece of paper. His secretary had thought it was funnier than most that came that way, and had laid it out in the place of honor. He read it absent-mindedly, crumpled it, and threw it into the empty wastebasket. But as he turned to the rest of his mail, lying there in an orderly pile, his mind suddenly registered what he had read, and he picked it out again, and smoothed it with his fingers.

Staring a long time at Fanya's handwriting, he smiled, and opened a drawer, and put the piece of paper away.)

* * *

Fanya was in the middle of washing when the letter was pushed under her door.

It made an important sound—in a house where letters come infrequently if they come at all, one of the most important sounds in the world.

Fanya heard it at once, and ran over just as she was, her wet fingers smearing the envelope when she picked it up.

She tore it open hastily. There was a poem inside . . . a poem based on the rhythm and phrasing of the line she had written.

"Generations of stifled words, reaching out *through you*
    Aching for utterance, dying on lips
That have died of hunger,
    Hunger not to have, but to be.

Generations as yet unuttered, dumb, inchoate,
    Unutterable by me and mine
In you I see them coming to be,

Luminous, slow-revolving, ordered in rhythm.
You shall not utter them; you shall be them.
    And from out thy pain
A song shall fill the world.

And I, from afar shall see
    As one watching sees the star
Rise in the waiting heavens,
    And from the distance my hand shall clasp yours,
And an old world be content to go,
    Beholding the horizon
Tremulous with the generations of the dawn."

She sat down on the bed and read it over three or four times. Her body grew cold and stiff, as the water dried on it, and at last she got up to finish her washing.

It was then she saw another piece of paper lying on the floor, which had dropped unnoticed from the envelope in her hurried opening of it.

Written in pencil, it must have been put in at the last moment—

"Won't you come and see me again. H. S."

*   *   *

"Your story affects me so deeply," he said when she came to see him. "You have flashed a light on a life which to most of us is obscure, if not wholly sealed. I can only say I have read it. It has become a part of me. You have made me live your life."

He looked at her for a long moment. Then, turning toward the window, he said, "It's so seldom one finds anyone as natural as you are. Direct, honest expression of feeling is not common. We are afraid to be ourselves. Even when we want to talk, we can't. We have lost the power to express any emotion naturally."

He with his great mind, afraid to be himself!—confiding to her his inadequacy. She listened to him in wondering silence.

"You make me realize that I have never really lived. My life is an evasion from life. It is not only that I have the habits of generations of repression to overcome, but I have the paths beaten out in my brain by the many years of intellectualizing."

His voice lowered; he seemed to have shocked himself with this breakdown of his reserve.

"You see, my whole tradition—our code—is to subject feeling to reason. Deny feeling till it ceases to exist."

At sight of her grave, earnest face, a half bantering smile came into his eyes. He leaned forward, gave her hand a friendly little pat.

"I don't want to inflict my moods on you. It seems to be a tragedy of life that no one can work himself out alone. It has to be always at someone else's expense."

He paused. "I am talking about myself. But as for you—I want you to feel that anything I can do is yours. And by the way," he announced, "there's a job for you. Our research bureau needs a Polish interpreter."

He turned to her, his face alight with enthusiasm.

"Do you realize that this is a turning point in your life? Till now, you've spent yourself; but in doing so, you've accumulated a capital of rich experience which is beginning to yield you interest. From now on you'll have time to write. Your struggling days are over. Now you will see an order and a meaning in everything that has ever happened to you. The events that have seemed a blur, a confusion, and a muddled failure, you will recreate in terms of art. For art is the climax of human experience."

He remained thoughtful for a moment, staring in abstraction at the ceiling. Fanya, watching him, wondered, why do people think of beauty and magnetism as the monopoly of youth? The lovers in books, the heroes on the screen—all of them young men. His face, warm and mellow as autumn, put to shame the vanity of the young.

"The investigation will not begin for some weeks. In the meantime—" he halted. "I want you to spend the time writing." A longer, more diffident, pause. "I have just been paid for an article, and this money would leave you free to devote yourself to your real work."

He dug his hand into his pocket and put on the table all the bills he seemed to have with him.

At the look in her face, he added, "Come, don't exaggerate the plan I'm proposing. I merely see an opportunity of placing a steadying hand at your elbow and helping you across a crowded street—being perhaps a little more familiar with the crowded traffic than you are. Many others would be glad to do the same thing. It's just my good fortune to be the first to see the opportunity."

He rose and put out his hand.

"I consider it a favor to be counted worthy to help you in any of the thousand ways in which one can help another. So there you are! Whatever I can do is yours to command."

He walked to the door with her and turned and smiled toward her, warmly.

"We have a tremendous lot to do together, haven't we?"

CHAPTER IV

Fanya spread a newspaper over her trunk, and put down bread, butter, and jam for her supper. On the scorched windowsill, water for the tea was heating in a tomato can set on a rusty gas-plate.

As she spread the jam over her bread, a sigh of pleasure and plenty escaped from her heart.

The room was not much to boast of. An iron cot, a chair, a shelf with hooks, about which hung a faded sickly pink curtain, improvised into a clothes closet. Her books, her papers, in grocery boxes on the floor, under a dilapidated, deal table whose glued legs wobbled and threatened to collapse whenever she leaned on it.

She was thinking of Scott; wondering if he would ever come so far to see her; wanting him to come, now that this mood of contentment was on her.

Suddenly she became aware of the smell of gas from the leaking stove, and she opened the door to air the room.

There he was—coming across the hall. She stood still, her hand at her throat, wondering at the inexplicable communication that had brought him to her at the very moment when she wanted him.

He took her hands in his, enjoying the wordless pleasure in her eyes.

"This very instant, I was thinking of you..."

"That's why I'm here."

He stared into the room then; and she caught the look of surprise and embarrassment on his face, before he had time to conceal it.

"You like my room?" She couldn't resist the question. "Well, you must. Because I like it today."

"I..." He glanced at the jumble of groceries on the trunk. "You're having supper?"

"I was just starting..."

"And is that all...bread and jam?"

"What's wrong with bread and jam? There's butter too—and tea—"

"You ought to have steak, salad, soup, vegetables..."

"I could have them. I could have bought anything with the money you gave me, but I can't get used to too much all at once."

He looked down at her, his brows drawn into a knot of pain.

"It hurts me when you tell me things like that. I couldn't eat my supper thinking of you. I had to come. Quick, Fanya, and put this away, and come to dinner with me."

"Oh-h!" Warm color flushed her face. Her lips parted but she could not speak. She turned to the window to force back the foolish tears...tears because she was too happy.

Spreading a towel over the food to keep the flies away, she put on her hat and coat, humbly surrendering to his dictatorship.

In the restaurant he watched her eat with the

delight of a thirsty man quenching his thirst at a clear brook.

The waiter kept putting food before her. Soup, chops, endive salad, ice cream. It was all part of the blurred mist of enchantment his presence created. His eyes upon hers as he drank a cup of coffee and smoked a cigarette.

The waiter and the cashier at the desk smiled after them as they left the restaurant.

A tide seemed to bear them along the street. They went on walking side by side, without touching or turning to each other.

"Where are we going?" she whispered.

He drew her hand within his arm, keeping his own hand tightly over it. "Let's walk."

"But you said you're behind in your work—"

"Work can wait. A night like this doesn't come often."

He turned to her suddenly.

"Take me to your ghetto. I want to see your ghetto and see it through your eyes."

It was a warm summer evening. Sidewalks and gutters were jammed with people. Men and women sprawled about on stoops, leaned out of windows. A hurdy-gurdy played. Children danced. Housewives haggled at the pushcarts.

A woman sat on a doorstep nursing her baby. Shop girls, chiffoned and rouged, tapped impatient feet, waiting restlessly for their beaux to bring to them the brief excitement of their evening. A white-bearded prophet sat in a group of old men expounding the

meaning of a passage in the Cabbala. Pushcart peddlers and hucksters vied with each other, shouting
their wares above the din of traffic and the shrieking
laughter of the dancing children. The street roared
like a carnival.

"There's richness and color for you!" Henry Scott's
eyes widened at the seething pageant spread before
him. He turned to Fanya, his low monotone accentu-
ated by gaiety. "They push out the walls of their homes
to the street. They live their family life in the open."

"No privacy. That's the worst of being poor."

Fanya pointed to the tenement canyons, alive with
peering faces. "The hours upon hours these women
waste just looking out of the windows."

"That's not wasting time. They're watching life go
by. There's an Oriental richness in their passivity."

The crowd swept them on to Seward Park. There
was to be music that evening. To get a seat near the
grandstand, people were coming hours ahead of time.
While waiting for the program to begin, children in
rags offered free entertainment, diving and splashing
in the stone fountain. Old people smiled indulgently
as they watched them play.

"These children have a curious magic in them. They
have turned that fountain into a beautiful thing."

"They have turned you into a sentimentalist," Fanya
said, but she smiled warmly at him, so that he did not
mistake her meaning.

One youngster, excited with the joy of the water,
took off his little shirt, squeezed it into a ball, and
hurled it at Scott.

He gasped at sight of his white linen splashed with mud. The next instant he burst into laughter, hurling it swiftly back at the boy. A circle of boisterous children and grown-ups surrounded them, watching the play.

"How these little loafers take to you!" Fanya laughed. "There must be a Jewish strain mixed in you somehow, or how could you feel so at home with them?"

"If I'm a Jew, you're a Yankee," he flashed back.

From out the shadow of a grimy, twisted tree, a dark-bearded Jew leaned his somber face over a basket of yellow pears. The man's eyes gazed into space millions of miles away from his body.

"There's a living Rembrandt for you," Scott whispered. To Fanya's amazement, he stopped to ask, "How much are the pears?"

"Two for a nickel."

The man reached for a bag, but Scott refused it; he gave one pear to Fanya and bit into the other.

"Look at yourself, eating unwashed fruit from a peddler in the street," she teased. How quickly the habits of his culture dropped away in his swift response to the people. "If you don't watch out, you'll be eating herring and onions yet."

He laughed softly into her eyes. Gathering the swarming warmth of the street in his voice, he said, "Who knows? Who knows what you may bring me to?"

The crowd grew more dense. A squad of policemen appeared suddenly to keep order. There was an audible hush. The band had arrived. In breathless suspense they waited for the music to begin.

The leader of the band rose, raised his baton. Silence. And then from the violins rose, as from far away, the first strains of Tchaikovsky's Symphony Pathetique. The closely packed park widened itself into a profounder silence. The people lifted their parched faces toward the magic shower of sound and let it fall upon them like rain long prayed for. Bowed backs straightened. Fear and worry dropped from their eyes. Released from the squalor and filth of the tenements they passed on through the gates of music into that other world which forever haunted their exiled lives.

At the end of the number there was a chance to squeeze through the aisle and out of the park.

"What is it that your people possess?" he asked, turning to Fanya on their way home. "What is this intensity which they carry into everything they do? The way they listen to music. The way the children dance and play. The way the housewives haggle at the pushcarts. The way your young men and women vitalize the air in my classrooms?"

"What is it?" Fanya caught at his arm as though to force an answer out of him. "Tell me! Tell me!"

"It seems to me the thing that gives them this amazing unity, the thing that drives them in all they do, is a deep thirst for life."

He looked through her into the far history of her people.

"There's an imprisoned splendor about your ghetto. This imprisoned splendor released—is what made the poets and artists of your race."

She fell into a silence, regarding him with a gaze wide as light. The night, the stars, the men and women who passed them by seemed to deepen the meaning of his words.

She had taken him to see the East Side with a sneaking sense of apology for her people, and he had made her feel proud to be one of them. He had made her see through the dirt and the poverty into their hearts, until the ghetto rose before her, a city set on a high hill whose light could not be hid.

"You wanted to see the ghetto through my eyes and ended by making me see it through your eyes. My old world is so fresh and new to you that it has become fresh and new to me."

Her voice lowered. She did not look at him. "How quickly those little roughnecks played ball with you! And that old Rembrandt of a peddler. How his face lighted when you stopped to buy his pears! You were never meant to be a professor in a college. You should have been a wandering beggar, a lover of the poor, like St. Francis of Assisi."

He smiled indulgently, caught up by her voice, the energy that poured out of her as she talked.

"I should never have seen your people as I've seen them tonight, if not for you. I shall always see your ghetto more vividly because of you. And you more vividly because of your ghetto."

CHAPTER V

He called her on the phone a few days later to tell her that he was leaving for Chicago. Even his absence was as it should be. She needed time to take in all that had happened to her since meeting him. He had given her back her own reality, but he was not quite real to her yet. Perhaps in this pause, this solitude, she could explain it to herself and to him.

"When I try to tell you of my gratitude, my lips are dumb," she wrote. "Perhaps I ought to be silent and still. Nothing but silence and stillness can voice that which I ache to say to you, but I must speak, even though speech is so inadequate.

"I have learned to abase myself. Now I must learn to abound. But want, want, want has so eaten itself into my bones—I do not know how to abound.

"Unhappiness, misery—they're like old clothes that fit me. But joy and gladness are like silk and satin instead of the coarse cotton I'm used to. And so you must forgive me if, when I try to tell you how I rejoice, I can only weep and thrust on you the shadow of my unreasonable sorrow.

"Tell me, how can I learn to work calmly? I have that aching sense of being in debt for this free time. How shall I ever make good to you my freedom? And yet—I can think of no deeper happiness on earth than to be indebted to you."

His answer came by the morning mail:

Dear Love of God,

I have your note, beautiful as your soul. I envy you. You are an artist and can say what need be said. You speak of being dumb when you are eloquent with the beauty of the world. It is I who am dumb, because I have never learned to speak. Perhaps I was born with the power but allowed it to be tied while you are translucent, and the world's own understanding and love shine through you.

Sometimes you will voice the injustice, the seeming injustice of things. It is you who suffer, while happiness comes to me. You who are young and powerful, alive for the world, and should have the world alive in you. While in my twilight, a beautiful garden with the brightness and perfume distilled from all the ages is suddenly opened to me. I know too well how the advantages are cruelly on my side. It is foolish to say do or don't to anybody, but nonetheless when you say you weep, I must say don't. My heart weeps that I cannot be with you and help you bear up. You need to be buoyed up and my arm should be sustaining you. And I know well that you weep because you have not been cared for in the past. You have not had sufficient food to keep your strength and it is undermined. You should be taken somewhere in the country where spring is coming and made to rest and be fed beefsteak and eggs and whatever is nourishing. You do not know how much of your present suffering is the revulsion of nature against the lack of physical basis for the ardent life of thought and emotion that you live. I have the feeling that you do not think sufficiently of your body, that you are inclined to think of such things as mundane and to be considered last, after other, more important matters are attended to. But your body is the bearer of your soul, and deserves all the care that the bearer of beautiful thoughts and feeling can have.

You ask how you can learn to work calmly. I am glad that you ask, though I cannot answer. But since you have begun to ask you will soon find the answer yourself. In time your body will discover what your soul already knows, that it is free, that you are not just having a reprieve from prison, but are out, once and forever. What you have to say will be said. What you have to do will be done. You cannot hurry, nor keep back. Live in peace and confidence. Anxiety to produce is not for you. Time is of God just as your freedom is. Why should you be anxious when and how God will use it?

I wonder if you know how much you have proved your right to pursue *your* writing, not only your right, but *the right*? So when you tell me that when you try to speak of gratitude your lips are dumb, do you not see what it means? Of course they are dumb. Your real you knows what you call your indebtedness to me is not to me at all; it is to the surprised wonder that such things can happen, and a thankfulness to the universe, to all nature, that it is as it is. Is it not thus, my strange, stranger friend? Such debts are indeed a promise of eternity—and that eternity is the leisure that your harassed body does not allow you to realize as yours. Yours because it belongs to you. Do not allow your body to make you feel that this leisure is only temporary, and therefore to be crowded with work. Your work is your leisure and your leisure your work. Henceforth God has all the time there is, and that completeness, that fullness of the moment is the only eternity.

I have much to say to you. When I see you, I'm too awkward to say it. I might feel freer to write, but I'm afraid the written word would be clumsy in another way. If I wasn't there to correct the false impression I had given. And I know you better than you know me. I am older. You know the old man in *Pelléas and Mélisande*—when I think of you and your suffering, I feel like him. It seems when one is old enough to understand, one can no longer do anything. And so it is that suffering comes to you when it ought to be happiness, while I, who could stand the suffering because I can see more than I can feel, get only the happiness. But you should not suffer as if you were dumb and stifled. You are beautifully communicative in simply being. You *are*, but you don't yet fully know that you are. You feel as if you wanted to be. You suffer from striving, but it is unnecessary. *You are already.* And perhaps I can have the great happiness of helping you to a realization that *you are*, and *what you are.* You do not have to reach, or strive, or try to achieve or accomplish. You already are. I repeat it a million times to you, my dear spirit. It only remains for you to do, and in order to do what you need most is material, earthly food, comfortable surroundings. All things of the spirit are yours, now.

CHAPTER VI

Is absence of a few days lengthened into weeks.
But she felt no separation. She wrote to him more
freely than she could have spoken to him.

At last he came back. On the way to his office, she
visualized how he would look at her. What he would
say. The way she would answer. Would there ever be
an end to the myriad things she had yet to tell him?

When he opened the door for her, she seized his
hand in both hers and held it without a word. In happy
silence, she sat down and faced him.

"I want to tell you something—" he paused and
looked at her, shy, diffident—unable to go on.

"Well?" She laughed her joy into his troubled eyes.
This great man so unsure of himself. The inimitable
hesitation of his speech! He seemed to obliterate himself before her so as to give her more courage to be
herself. Just as adults do with children they love. What
was the secret of his rare humility—the power that
enabled him to make of himself a background that lit
her into shining life?

"I went away," he said, in a very low voice, "because—
because I didn't feel sure of myself."

She looked at him, questioning.

"That last Sunday—our visit to the ghetto—" Again

he paused, his voice almost inaudible. "It was all bloom and fragrance. I want to keep that fragrance. Not spoil it. Do you see what I mean?"

Her hands moved tensely over the arms of her chair, but no word came to her lips.

His eyes pleaded for understanding. He waited. After a long silence he said, "I went away because—"

"Why? Why?" she cried, suddenly finding her voice.

"Well—don't you understand? I was afraid—"

"Afraid of what?"

"Afraid of myself."

"Why?" she persisted.

He crumpled in his chair. He seemed to grow small and helpless—his body emptied of himself.

Suddenly a new light flashed into his eyes. "You said that night that I gave you back the meaning of your race. Now it is I who ask for understanding. I am an old-fashioned, Yankee puritan. I do not belong to myself—"

A long pause.

And then he drew from his pocket a worn bundle of letters. Her letters.

"Keep these for me. Will you?"

A puzzled frown gathered between her brows.

"Don't you want them?"

"Yes. I want them, but you keep them for me."

Her eyes swept the deep drawers of his desk, the tall files, and then back to his troubled eyes.

"Why can't you keep them?"

"Because I do not belong to myself."

"It's fear," she burst out. "You fear to feel. You fear to suffer—"

"No. I was only trying to save you from finding me out."

His gaze sought hers, but she kept staring at the bundle of letters.

"Maybe you know best," he said humbly. "Too much wisdom makes fools of the wise. Perhaps your instinct may be surer than all my reasoning."

She kept staring at her letters with unseeing eyes. Folding and unfolding them, unaware what her hands were doing.

"Remember what I tell you now, in a comparative moment of sanity," he went on. "You suffer infinitely more than I do, but at least you have unity. I am always fighting myself. My cursed analytical mind keeps me running away from myself—intellectualizing—generalizing. You must not be impatient with me."

Disregarding his words, she put the letters in her purse, talking to herself, "This is murder. Murder for the sake of safety."

"I was only trying to protect you—"

"I do not want to be protected," she burst out fiercely. "I want to live. I want the sun to shine. I want the sap to flow. I want life. Life in all its terribleness—in all its suffering. But not safety. Not death."

At the door, she said simply, "You don't want to see me any more?"

"How can I help wanting to see you? I need you. You are fire and sunshine and desire. You make life full of daily wonder."

*   *   *

In spite of his reassuring words, there were the letters he had returned. An invisible cloud of darkness
pushing them apart. She tried to reason the darkness
away, to see and feel only his eyes, following her—
pleading for understanding.

For thousands of years, his race and hers were fear-
ing, mistrusting, hating, and fighting each other. And
for the first time, here in America, they met face to
face. Was it a wonder that the ancient battle had thrust
its shadow of doubt and fear between them?

The world of hope that had driven her to him, the
miracle of his response, the revelation of their visit to
the ghetto—was fear and doubt and mistrust to be the
fruit of it all?

In that interlude of light, she felt his presence very
near, very real. Henry Scott had a fragrance of something higher and finer than any man of her own race
she had ever known. He was the promise of the centuries. The ancient discord between Gentile and Jew
crashing through into rarest harmony.

A great, unutterable need for him took possession of
her. She wanted to go to him now. Never did such hunger, such longing sweep her as the hunger and longing
for him at that moment. But she sat there in her room,
unstirring—unmoving—instead of jumping up and has-
tening to him as she wanted to do. Something was holding her back. And she wondered afterwards whether it
wasn't her instinct that he was even then coming toward
her. He seemed coming closer and closer. Everything
about him was so miraculous. She was scarcely surprised when she heard his knock at the door.

It was like the silent force of unvoiced prayer to see him suddenly before her eyes.

He put down a small satchel and a bundle of newspapers he carried and took a seat on the trunk, facing her.

"I have such good news for you. I had to come."

"Tell me! Tell me!" she cried, catching the gay ring in his voice, the gleam of his eyes. "Quickly—please !"

"Wait a moment, Fanya!"

"Oh you—you—you old-fashioned Yankee! You awful puritan!" She thrust the words at him with reckless abandon.

"What's that?" He frowned with mock disapproval. "You new, undisciplined daughter of the ghetto!" She loved him for the difficulty he found in playing with her. Then with an assumption of official dignity, he unwrapped the bundle of Polish newspapers and handed them to her.

Bewildered, she looked at the papers and then at him. "Why? What is it?"

"From now on you are employed as the official translator of the Polish research bureau," he announced.

Never before had she seen him so happy except on their visit to the ghetto when he played with the children in the street and hobnobbed with the pushcart peddlers.

"The study in Chicago will not begin for another month," he went on. "But your translation is advance work upon which we'll base our study. You'll have to decide what is important for us to know."

There was in his voice the breathless jubilance of a child giving a cherished present to one he loved.

"My dear, what makes me so happy is that it isn't just another job, but the kind of work that will stimulate your writing. And your writing is your real life, Fanya. Everything changes and passes away. But art endures; because art is the marriage of the personal to the eternal."

Her hands moved tensely in her lap. Her intent eyes fastened on his. How he could feel when he let himself go! How selfless his feelings were! His deepest joy always in other people.

Was that why his race walked about in such a stiff armor of restraint? What Jew or Slav could feel as intensely as an Anglo-Saxon when he sheds his rigid puritan pose?

"I believe you'll need this," he said, setting the satchel on the table and opening it.

"Oh!" She looked at a shining, new typewriter. "Will I ever learn to type my stuff?"

"Sit right down," he commanded.

She sat down, smiling. "How shall I begin?"

"Isn't there something you want to transcribe?"

She picked up a page from a loose manuscript and read to him the first sentence from it. "'Like all people who have nothing, I lived on dreams.' —Do you like it?"

"Yes," he nodded.

"Oh you!" she chided gaily. "How can you ever teach me anything, Henry? When you approve of everything I say?"

"But I do approve, Fanya. If I could only make you believe enough in yourself—make you aware of your own ability."

Her laughing eyes darkened, humbled before his selfless devotion.

"You don't really flatter people," she said in a very low voice, unconsciously falling into his mellowed monotone. "You draw out their powers because you honestly believe in them. Isn't that the essence of all your teaching, in all your books? Your faith in people?"

"There is in human nature a need for courage, for faith. And whoever builds on that, builds on a fundamental truth."

"Just the same," Fanya insisted, "I can no longer depend on you as a critic—"

"It's true," he confessed. "I love everything you say and the way you say it so much that I've lost the power to criticize you dispassionately."

"I wonder why I still have power to criticize you dispassionately? Is it because fools rush in where wise men fear to tread?" She laughed into his eyes. "I guess my ignorance gives me poetic license to find flaws with the master."

"I'll not have you call yourself ignorant." He took her hand strongly in his and held it. "I want your criticism. I need it. Haven't I told you at the very beginning that you can do more for me than I can ever do for you?"

"Well then, if you want the truth, Henry"—she paused, groping for words, "your book *The Meaning of Democracy* belies the title. It's written in such abstract, undemocratic language nobody but a handful of college people can make head or tail out of it. Whenever I try to read it, I get so lost under the heavy weight of words—" She broke off and looked at him with pleading in her eyes. "That book was meant to be the Bible of America. It's wicked not to have it available for everybody. You could light up the lives of millions. But somehow it needs flesh and blood."

He drew a diagram and then explained it to her. On one side was he, trying to build a bridge of understanding between the different races and nations of the world. He could not reach everybody so he talked only to specialists, engineers of education who in turn would interpret him to the masses.

"The essence of my book on Democracy simply means that we all need each other," he went on. "The battle between races and classes and creeds is but the struggle of man to understand himself. As we grow to know ourselves, we grow into a deeper appreciation of others who are different."

Her arms rushed out to him in a swift gesture, as though to gather his thought to her before it vanished in the air.

"Why can't you write your books just the way you are talking to me now?" she cried imploringly.

"A philosopher must present his ideas in the language of philosophy which must be learned by those who wish fully to understand him. So I speak to a small group—"

"Oh! Your engineers of education," she flung at him impatiently. "Don't you see that you yourself refute your own ideas of democracy? You talk about breaking down barriers between people and you begin by talking in a language that needs a dictionary and arid intellectuals for interpreters."

Suddenly touched by his patience, his gentle for-bearance with her roughness, she said in a softened voice, "You can present your ideas in the simple lan-guage of the people. I have your letters to prove it."

She looked far out—stern forehead, exultant eyes, seeing prophecies. "In your books you are an intellect talking to scholars. In your letters you are—you are—St. Francis, loving the poor—Christ on the mountain, blessing the multitude."

"I love your image of me which is not me," he said, surrendering to the disturbing delight of her enthusi-asm. "I love it, because you see it in me."

He went on, more to himself than to her: "I am in you that too beautiful idealization of myself which I admire and love—but am not. It is not storm and clouds and daring you bring me, but down to earth that is mother, cradle, home, and grave of us all. Earth that gives us peace and rest in her arms."

He broke off, as he felt her rapt scrutiny, and smiled at her as a child smiles at another, sharing a mutual joy.

"I suppose my rambling doesn't sound like sense at all. But I feel you understand me, somehow—not that understanding is always necessary."

She was so lost in the music of his voice that she did not hear a word of what he was saying. And they just looked at each other without saying anything.

CHAPTER VII

The members of the research group were renting a house in the Polish district of Chicago where they could stay while the investigation was being carried on.

"I'm frightened at the thought of living under one roof with your engineers of education," she said to him in sudden doubt of herself. "Do you think doctors of philosophy and I can mix together?"

"Of course you can. When you pool your ideas on actual problems, all differences will serve only to enrich the work."

As she sat there in his office, a dark-haired, attractive girl came in. Fanya noted the graceful set of her shoulders and the poise of her walk.

"Professor Scott," she asked, smiling, "I want to know what you think of my thesis?"

"It has been accepted," he said briefly. And then, turning to Fanya, "Miss lvanowna, meet Miss Foster, the other woman of our study group."

Miss Foster, with her freshly-minted Ph.D. and Fanya, slightly self-conscious, looked at each other appraisingly.

"How nice that there will be another woman," Miss Foster offered politely.

"I'm so anxious for the work to begin," said Fanya. And added, with her cursed ghetto humility, "I feel so awfully inadequate compared to a trained person like you."

At Miss Foster's complacent acceptance of her remark, she immediately regretted it.

"I told you, Fanya, you have something that trained people lack," Henry put in, smoothing the awkward pause.

She met two others that afternoon in his office. Robert Drake, the chairman of the group, a scholarly young professor of philosophy, in horn-rimmed glasses, and Henry Edman, a sociology instructor with a brilliant self-assurance.

"How do you like them?" he asked, after they were gone.

"You'd better tell me if they like me," she countered. "I'm so drawn to you cold Anglo-Saxons. It's as though my soul were in your soul, but you always thrust me out, at arm's length." There was a baffled, frustrated note in her voice. "Why do I need them so terribly, when they don't need me?"

"Give them time, Fanya," he admonished. "You have just been introduced to them. You can't expect a full-blown flower of intimacy and affection when you have but just planted a seed."

His words switched her back to her thwarted encounter with the Farnsworths six years ago, and she told him of her blundering letter.

"Why didn't they answer me?"

"Perhaps they were too embarrassed to know how to answer you," he explained. "The Farnsworths have

been brought up for generations in the belief that
any display of emotion is vulgar. Your fire frightened
them."

His eyes held hers for a long moment of silence and
then his gaze turned to the window. "They were afraid
they'd have to give themselves too deeply to you. They
wanted to treat you kindly, but not intimately—"

"Cruel kindness!" she burst out. "Why put on this
shining cloak of benevolence—inviting a shop girl to
a Thanksgiving dinner—not out of the need to share,
but to amuse themselves, to enjoy the pleasure of
entertaining an alien. Then, when they're satisfied
with their momentary sensation of being kind—they're
through—and want no more of you."

She flung out her arms in one of her vivid, startling
gestures. "It's like holding up water to lips perishing
from thirst—and then withdrawing the cup. Like leading a homeless man to the threshold of home—and
then shutting the door in his face."

Instead of the sympathy she had expected, she
heard his low, chuckling laughter.

"What is it you're laughing about?" she demanded.

"How can I help laughing at your damned Slavic
seriousness? In your passion for tragedy you make a
mountain out of a molehill. It hurts your vanity to realize that you've been a fool to let yourself be wounded
by the Farnsworths, so you strike out blindly at them
and attribute to them motives unworthy of your intelligence. Do you remember the time you took me to your
ghetto, and one of the little rough necks, splashing in
the fountain, took off his shirt and threw it in my face,

spattering mud all over me? What would you have thought of me if I had become angry? I laughed it off. You must learn to laugh, Fanya—"

"I can't laugh. I won't laugh. I'm the product of abused generations that had laughter squeezed out of them."

She rose and walked over to the window. Why had he never invited her to his home—introduced her to his wife, his sons, his daughters? He befriended her on the side. He wrote her wonderful letters—divine poetry, but when it came to taking her into his home— accepting her as a social equal—he, too, had his reservations. Even he had for her only a cruel kindness, like the Farnsworths.

As if sensing the cold wave of her thoughts, he turned to her.

"If you want to understand people, you must stop blaming them for being what they are and the way they are. Your attitude should be that of an explorer, exploring a strange country, surrounded by strange animals. You must study your animals—what makes them bite and what makes them come to you. Nobody's ways are any better than anybody else's, but if you happen to migrate into a foreign country, you must learn the ways of its people. Learn to give what you want to give them in their terms."

Elbows resting on her knees, she sat staring before her. Her puzzled solemnity made him unusually communicative.

"Have you ever taken care of a cat or a dog?" he asked, trying to rouse her from her stony mood.

"I don't know what you're driving at. I never had a pet."

"Think of a child growing up without a pet!" He looked at her in amazement, touched by her barren childhood. "Well, the difference between a cat and a dog is this: Both of them want to be loved like every other thing alive, but they don't like the same way of having love shown to them. You can hug a dog all day long and he'll come back begging for more. But a cat is an aesthete of affection. If you shower too much affection on a cat, it runs away and disappears. That's the nature of the animal. And you can't reason with animals. The Anglo-Saxon is another aesthete of affection."

As always, after they had fought through some disputed, vexed question, they fell into a silence. So deep, so wide was the give and take between them—always he had power to take from her the hurts that warped her spirit, her blind warring with the world—and give her his tolerance and his peace.

CHAPTER VIII

Fanya, with her grips in her hands, pushed through the scurrying throngs in Grand Central Station, looking for the track marked Chicago Express. Pausing at the information desk, she saw her new associates gathered in the waiting room. She waved excitedly as she came toward them, and, like a bad omen, the glued handle of the satchel came off, scattering her clothes all about her.

Chemise, tooth-brush, hairpins, and powder fell at the feet of Robert Drake, the solemn-faced professor of philosophy. He bent down politely to help her. After an embarrassing moment of forcing her things back into place, she looked up to meet their amused smiles.

Their luggage, though worn, was of such solid, good quality, it made her new, cheap imitation-leather ashamed of itself. Her quickly assembled outfit looked shoddy and vulgar against Miss Foster's quiet good taste. The open satchel had exposed her cotton underwear. A depressing sense of her difference from them checked her enthusiasm.

"How did you get into this work?" Fanya asked Miss Foster, after they settled themselves in the train.

"Oh, it was one of the first jobs to open up. A chance

to get some experience. Besides, I thought I might get quite a kick out of visiting the foreign homes."

So it was only a slumming adventure to her!

"Why did you take up sociology?"

"Well, I like it better than the other subjects I studied at college."

Noting the expression on Fanya's face, she added: "As a matter of fact, the girls I know who are in sociology are doing it to help those whom life has pinched harder than it has them."

The first day after they had located in Chicago, Fanya watched with vague misgiving the formidable reference books they arranged on the shelf and about the desks of their office.

"Why these millstones of learning?" She laughed, picking up one of the books.

"All these are on our bibliography list." Miss Foster handed Fanya the typewritten sheets.

Fanya glanced at the first lines: *Polish Peasant* by William Thomas. *Humanizing Education* by John Dewey. *Our Slavic Fellow Citizens* by Emily Balch....

"The titles alone stop my thoughts." She sighed, handing back the list.

"Well, what have you to suggest?" asked Miss Foster, bristling.

Fanya stared at her with bewildered eyes. It was one thing to decry their ready-made methods, but what had she to offer in their place? Her thoughts were deep inside her—complicated and confused. When she tried to get hold of what she thought, she felt the agony of an emotion without words.

"I don't know," Fanya fumbled. "But it seems to me to read about people you want to know is as different from knowing them as looking at the picture of an apple is different from the taste and feel of a real apple. Go out and meet the Poles—"

"Of course we'll do that, but first we must decide on methods of approach, how to gather our facts—"

"Facts?" she repeated, staring blankly at Miss Foster. "I wonder if I shall ever learn your scientific method of approach. It seems to me you must feel first what people love and admire—to know them."

"Emotional ecstasy gets you nowhere. A scientific research must be impersonal, objective. Facts of wages, occupations, housing conditions—"

With a shrug of her shoulders Fanya turned to her desk and began straightening out her papers.

Miss Foster—with her smooth, sure face, and the clear, confident gaze of her eyes—fitted so beautifully into this world. All her education, her training was to save her from looking into the depths where things get complicated and unutterable.

At their ten o'clock conference, a file of Polish newspapers was handed to Fanya, as her day's work. Before she started with her translations, the others reported abstracts of their reading and the contacts made the previous day. Miss Foster read an interview with the social worker who had told her of some of the interesting "cases" of the neighborhood. There followed an account of a talk with a priest, another with a schoolteacher. The social worker with her "cases," the priest with his parish, the teacher with her class—all glibly forgetting the individual in their abstractions. The Poles were to them people outside themselves. Specimens, types they could tabulate and pigeonhole in their daily reports. But to Fanya, the Poles were a living part of herself. The more she thought about them, the less she could express herself in words. She turned to her newspapers. It was just another day's toil. Laboring with the unreal—because the real evaded her grasp.

At dinner, when they were exchanging funny incidents of the day, one of the men told how he went with the visiting teacher to a ditch digger's home. They found the baby's tin bathtub being used for a garbage pail.

"Mrs. Janowich!" exclaimed the horrified teacher. "Baby's bathtub must never be used for dirt."

Whereupon the mother explained," The baby is two years old already and don't need baths any more."

They broke into roars of laughter.

"I've got one better," came from Miss Foster. With marvelous power of mimicry, she related the way an old Polish peasant woman came weeping into the settlement because her daughter, who had just begun to work as a stenographer, had left home. The sudden wealth of her own wages had gone to her head, and she refused to sleep in the same room as her three brothers. "But seriously speaking," Miss Foster concluded, "doesn't this illustrate the point in Siegfried's *America Comes of Age*—the conflict of standards between the first and the second generation of immigrants? We ought to make a note of this."

"Oh, let's stop talking shop!" one of the men put in. "Enough to carry the Poles on our backs all day long. I'm for union hours."

The conversation drifted to the latest show. They glanced through the amusement column to decide where they were to go that evening. Then the chairman held up the front page, with a picture of Henry Scott just as he was about to board a train.

"Did you notice the picture of the chief today? His shoelace dangling loose as usual. I never saw a man of his position so careless about his appearance. Either his coat is stained or his trousers in need of pressing—"

"They say his wife has to hand him clothes or he'd forget to put them on," came from one of the men. "One day, while his wife was gone, he came to the lecture hall without his necktie."

"I wonder what the old man is like personally?" someone asked.

"No one knows him personally," put in Miss Foster. "He's as dry and dull and bloodless as he is at his seminars." And she told how, when he gave her a passing mark on her thesis, she went up to him and asked how he liked it.

"'Your thesis has been accepted,' he grunted. And that was all I could get out of him."

Each member of the group knew something about him and was eager to relate it.

"Professor Thornton says he visited the chief forty years ago when his kids were small. He found the four of them sitting on top of him, playing he was their donkey. The kids never called him father, but just plain

'Henry' and treated him as though he was a mat under their feet."

"Say!" one of the men grinned. "Have you ever met that young Spaniard he adopted? Well, they say that's one of his illegitimate sons. While he was on a visit to Spain, he fell in love with a Spanish peasant woman and he brought the little brat as a present to his wife."

"Well, the old boy was no St. Anthony in his day. And even now—women go nuts over him. All the women painters are wild to paint his picture. And every sculptress wants to model his head."

Fanya twisted her shoulders and looked embarrassed and unhappy as the conversation went on.

"I pity his poor wife," sighed Miss Foster. "Someone who is an intimate friend of theirs said—that when the journal of Tolstoy's wife was published, Mrs. Scott said to someone at their dinner table that if she ever wrote up her life, as the professor's wife, it would beat anything Countess Tolstoy suffered at the hands of Tolstoy." She paused, and then, "Great men are incapable of love," she declared. "Their intellectual egotism prevents them from being dominated by any personal emotion."

"He's not as innocent as he's cracked up to be," said the chairman. "I heard one of his colleagues say he's the shrewdest Yankee going. He's gotten more publicity than any other professor at the university. He knows how to keep himself in the public eye."

"He loathes the limelight," Fanya said, hotly.

"Does he? Then why is his picture in the papers all the time?"

There was a strained silence. Then Henry Edman jumped up on the chair.

"Ladies and gentlemen," he announced, "may I conclude the discussion of our chief with an impersonation of our esteemed interpreter, Fanya Ivanowna?" He clasped his hands at his heart. "Note the passionate gesture. In the early hours of the morning, when our eyes are still heavy with sleep, our tragedy queen assaults the innocent mailman in a tragically tremulous voice, 'Is—there—any mail—for—me-ee?'" He mimicked Fanya in sepulchral tones. She smiled thinly, trying to join in their laughter.

Let them laugh. If they knew from whom those letters came...

CHAPTER IX

The questionnaire for gathering their facts was drawn up. Robert Drake began:

"Considering the purposes of our study, what is a workable hypothesis to keep in mind as we fill out our schedule?"

After days of discussion of the "workable hypothesis," "consistency and accuracy of data," the chairman concluded:

"Of course, you'll all bear in mind that anything you observe about the nature of these people, not covered in the questionnaire must be carefully noted. And now, are you all agreed that the field we have chosen is a representative sample, that it has all types and kinds of situations, and is inclusive of the whole population?"

"You'll never understand these people!" Fanya spoke up, trying to keep the edge out of her voice. "It can't be done so coldly."

There was a snap. A crossing of currents. A long moment of silence in which they looked at each other. After a pause, the chairman said in a very low voice, almost too low with restraint: "I do not believe your emotional attitude is desirable in our study. It's only as one works out details and facts that one can understand what is just and fair to do—"

"But what is just and fair to do? Why, that's the whole heart of it—and you—you—"

Unable to restrain her feelings she fled from the room.

Out on Michigan Avenue, a cool wind from the lake blew against her cheeks. She turned her face hungrily toward this merciful coolness.

The summer sunset hidden behind the towering cliff of buildings left only a blue wash of light on the wide street. Refreshed by the wind, the air, Fanya was suddenly alive to all that stirred about her.

A flock of pigeons winged out from the grimy, darkened cornices of the Art Institute. Undisturbed by the smoke, the clamor of the city below them, they wheeled serenely through the air. Watching the poised flight of the birds, Fanya knew the center of stillness which was one with the birds, the wind, the air.

What was this cloak of the flesh agitated always with surface trivialities? It was this excitable flesh, this thing of darkness that prevented her from living in the light within and about her. Prevented her from making those deeper contacts she longed for. It was this real part of herself that she wanted to bring, like a gift, to Henry Scott.

Calmed, self-possessed, she entered the Polish-American Club. The social room was deserted. Over in the corner, Fanya saw a phonograph. Selecting from a group of records Chopin's Nocturne in E flat, she set it in motion on the machine.

The clear, bell-like notes deepened her peace. The quarrel of the afternoon seemed as childish as it was

absurd. Through the pleading chords of this healing
nocturne, Fanya felt the differences that had separated her from her co-workers become magnets drawing her resistlessly toward them. In this moment of
nearness, she was closer to these strangers than to her
own kind.

"Well, has your Americanization bunch set the
world on fire yet?"

Fanya looked up. A blond, vivacious Pole sat down
beside her. The editor of one of the Polish newspapers.
"Whatever got you in with those hundred percenters—
those Saviours of Society?"

Fanya met the man's eyes from a long way off.

"Doesn't the whole thing strike you as rather
ridiculous?"

She looked out of the window. Slowly, passing her
hand over her hair, she turned her head back to him.

"Doesn't everything which we do not understand
seem to us ridiculous?"

"Do you mean to tell me you find anything real in
the cold-blooded studies of these sociologists?"

"You and I are so over-emotional, nothing seems
real to us but our own emotion." She paused, picking her words slowly, thoughtfully. "I wonder, is it our
envy of their steady disciplined energy, their power to
keep their heads over their hearts that makes us think
them cold-blooded and heartless?"

"But what right have they to come here and study
us? Suppose we turned around and studied them?"

"Well, why not?"

Other members of the club dropped in, moved over

to hear what the discussion was about. Before long a circle of men and women surrounded them.

"She works for that Americanization bunch," one man whispered scoffingly. "It's her pay-envelope. She's got to defend her job."

Fanya looked up. Her hands resting quietly upon the arms of the chair, she bent her tranquil face toward her listeners.

"Friends," she said, slowly, anxious not to blur her thought with the inadequacy of words, "I know how hard it is when you're up against the merciless struggle for bread—when you wear out body and brain to wrest a mere animal existence—I know how hard it is to believe that there is beauty and kindness and love in the world. But you all know that side by side with the ruthless fight for a living is the hunger in your heart for something more than bread and rent. So in this country, side by side with the might of money and the squalor of poverty—is the hunger in the hearts of the people for—for—" She paused, reaching out her hands to them in her dumbness. Her eyes burning into their eyes, "You know what this hunger is—"

They nodded back to her. As though in this gesture toward them she had torn open her heart and they had seen what lay so unutterably deep in her—in them.

Helped by their response, she went on. "America is different from the old, finished countries from which we come. America is a country still in the making. It is still in the process of growing. It has in it the splendor and the hope of youth. The big thing about America is what it might become. And it needs you and me, the last no less than the first, to make of it the country of promise it was meant to be."

She paused again, searching for words. Gathering fire out of their rapt faces.

"This research study is the first groping gesture toward the dream which you and I have dreamed. The dream that for hundreds of years, in thousands of starved villages in Poland, Russia, and Rumania, men have dreamed was America—"

"But why all this fancy language?" a man with high, Slavic cheekbones and a stubborn jaw broke in. "Will it help us to get jobs? I want work. Something that will help me pay rent."

The man's simple question shamed her out of her eloquence. Her hand went over her eyes as though to shut out the abyss of want that she saw in his grim, haunted face. The abyss from which she had but just escaped. By the mercy of Henry Scott, she had been given a moment's reprieve, and already she was justifying herself with the easy platitudes of those who have never known the struggle for bread.

"How could I answer you?" the cry broke from her. "God! Who could answer you?"

The audience drew back, waiting in silence for her to go on. She felt guilty, sentenced by this man for indulging in dreams. What were all the social studies worth that would improve things in ten or twenty years to this man who wanted work now?

"Of course this research is only an attempt to get at your problem," she said, again reaching toward them in her helplessness. "But *it is* an attempt. And it will go on and on, after us, till your question is answered."

"Write this for my paper," the editor exclaimed. "This man's question and your answer."

"But I have no answer," she shook her head sadly.

"I believe that you have," he said with conviction. "I must have it for next Sunday. And you must do it for me."

His belief in her swept away her doubts. "Yes. I will write it for your paper and for our group," she said, gathering up her things.

They crowded about to shake hands and thank her. Smiling and waving a swift good-bye, she hurried out, eager to write the article while the spell of their listening faces was still upon her.

She did not stop to have dinner, but went straight to the office. Opening the drawer for paper, she found a carbon copy of a letter addressed to Henry Scott:

Dear Mr. Scott,

I have been delegated by the members of our research group to write you about Miss Ivanowna. We have tried to explain to her the purpose and methods of our study, but she is not able to accept them. We appreciate the fact that Miss Ivanowna has had experience which should make her valuable as an interpreter, but her attitude is so destructively critical, and she colors all she observes with her own over-emotionalism so much that we feel we cannot depend on her observations as scientifically accurate. We fear she would infect the whole study with her persecution mania, her unfortunate psychosis. We regret to trouble you about this, but we feel you would want to know of our difficulty. We believe we must have another interpreter.

It was signed by the chairman.

Slowly, carefully, she put the letter back in the drawer. The long, summer twilight drifted into dusk. Fanya sat staring out of the window, unaware that the city had lighted a million lamps against the darkness.

There followed an interminable week of suspense in which Fanya waited for the worst to happen. One afternoon she had gone out on one of her long walks. A Pole, evidently a day laborer, stopped her, handed her a slip of paper, and asked her to read for him the address of an employment agency. As she directed him to the agency, he told her all about himself. He had to pay five dollars in advance, before he could get a job. Often it did not last more than a couple of weeks and he had to pay again for another job. "It's always pay, pay, in America. Even for a job."

The cry of this man's terrible need echoed the cry of that other man at the club. And there were hundreds, thousands like them. Human beings reduced by the cruelty of existence to a mere hunt for a job. In the face of such brutal want that clamored for immediate relief, how could one be calm and cool enough to carry on an impersonal, scientific social study? Could one who had come up out of this want ever achieve an impersonal attitude?

It had all seemed so clear when she had stood with the wind blowing against her, watching the flight of the birds; when she had listened to the music. But she had lost it somehow. Again Henry stood before her. He was the union of the personal and the impersonal. The head and the heart working in harmony. Was that the magic of his personality?

As she approached the door of the office, she stopped. He was there. With her hand against the wall, in an effort to get hold of herself, she heard him say, "No, we cannot dismiss her. Her viewpoint is so different, it will stimulate you to verify your own."

"But Professor Scott," the chairman broke in, "the woman is impossible. You don't know her."

"We tried to help her, telling her what to read," added one of the men. "But she not only refuses to read; she ridicules the textbooks to defend her ignorance."

"Well," returned Henry Scott, "if you cannot survive the ridicule of her ignorance—then your stand cannot be very sound."

They all laughed. Now the joke was on them, and even she could smile.

"People are not fixed objects, like tables or chairs," he went on. "The way in which you treat them and feel toward them—that's half of what they are to you. She represents the impatience with conventionality, that suffocating unwillingness to be held down by non-essentials which is exactly what we need to warm and animate our reasoning habits—

"America is not England. It cannot and it does not want to remain in what is vaguely called the Anglo-Saxon mold. If America is to be anything but a mass of warring elements, it must take into its very being the spiritual contributions of other races—of immigrants later than our own first wave."

"But look here, professor—" Robert Drake interposed, "the woman has no sense of proportion—no shading—no discrimination. She's like a drawing without perspective. Everything is just as important to her as everything else. She's just one red, hot fire of emotion."

"Yes," Henry admitted. "She is one red, hot fire. And where would we be without fire? What do sensible people do with fire? They don't turn their backs on it and go away. They try to get some of its vital heat and yet not get burned up by it. It seems to me as though that's the job of America in general and ours in particular."

This was followed by a low murmur of discussion. In that interval, Fanya summoned the courage to knock and walk in.

There was a nod of greeting. A pause, as he waited for her to be seated. Probably no one but she caught the quick color that flitted across his face. The swift flame like a living thing that leaped between them. None of this betrayed itself in the half-closed eyes, in the casual way he continued his low monotone.

"Now as to the questionnaire. From the report you sent and from our discussion today, I see you have made a thorough preliminary investigation, but I doubt if the questionnaire would be of any use."

He picked up the sample card that had just been brought from the printer.

"The Russell Sage Foundation has rooms stacked full of tabulated facts and they're not worth the paper they're written on. I call this sort of thing social busy work. We must find more vital methods of approach."

CHAPTER X

The group had arranged a theatre party for that evening, but Henry professed to be too tired from the journey to accompany them. After they had gone, Fanya found him in the office.

He put down his papers as though he had been waiting for her.

"I'm glad you have come, young lady," he bantered. "There is a good spanking in store for you."

He swung back in his chair, his hands deep in his pockets—pretending to look stern.

"You have been reported for insubordination. Whatever shall I do with you?"

"You might make me write a hundred times, 'I am an ignorant Bolshevik. I am an ignorant Bolshevik. I'm guilty of ridiculing the Scientific Method and the Holy Textbooks.'" She laughed, and he joined in the laughter.

He could still be facetious after all the trouble she had made.

"I deserve to have you hate me," she said, suddenly grave.

"Hate you!" His eyes, deep and wide with understanding, regarded her. All her faults blotted out in his forgiveness.

His hand stole over hers and rested there. What a warm, communicative hand! Like quicksilver. Life leaped through every pore of her being. He had the gift of communicating the unutterable by a look, a silence, a mere touch of his fingertips.

"I've been in that stuffy train so long," he said. "Let us go out to one of the parks for air."

So much there was to talk over. Only in the stillness of the open could she really feel free to talk.

But out in the street, when he took her arm with a friendly little gesture of instinctive fellowship, she forgot everything she had to say. She was unaware of the people they brushed by, the streets they were passing. Enchantment enveloped her like a cloud.

They turned into the park and walked down the graveled pathway. The light and shadows fell from the silent elms above them; they passed across the grass, touched gently by the quiet gold of the late afternoon light. They did not speak—the faint rustle of the burnished leaves above them might have been their voices, so close were they now to the beauty of all the world.

Far behind them was the city with its noise and crowds. They seemed all alone, at the edge of the earth. Before them the glory of sunset, like some cosmic ritual—a merging of the Unseen with the Unknown.

They leaned toward each other, his hand groping for her hand. He kissed her fingers one by one.

With her fingers drawn through his, they looked at each other, frankly, understandingly. Never had they been so happy together. And their happiness was in their eyes. Just to look at one another was bliss.

In the slowly silvering sky, the last pale tints of the sun's reflection drifted and died. Around them, as in answer to the daylight's last salutation, a little voice-less murmur came from the earth.

With a small sound of tenderness, he drew her to him. Silently she surrendered herself to his arms. He bent his head to hers and kissed her.

"Do you love me?" he whispered, drawing her closer to him, kissing her neck, her mouth with infinite caressiveness.

"Dearest!" Suddenly his lips pressed her lips with fierce insistence, his hand fumbling her breast. "My dearest one!" Hungry desire was in his voice—hunger old as the world. "Love me! Do you love me?"

A crashing of sights and sounds and feelings. Blind terror—confusion. The shattering impact of his lips thrust her from him even in his arms. Dark barriers rose inside her. They welled up in her heart—the sorrow—the disillusion! Instead of a god, here was a man—too close, too earthly. She wanted from him vision—revelation—not this—not this.

All at once, aware of her unresponsiveness, he released her. They stood awkwardly, looking away from each other. After a while, he turned to her gently, back in his habitual low monotone.

"Perhaps we had better go home."

She nodded.

A little chill breeze came out of the darkness. He drew away from her. Mechanically, she followed him. Her hair fluttered against her cheek. She did not brush it back.

They walked slowly homeward, each lost in his own thoughts. She glanced at him, timidly. His eyes were full of something going on inside his mind. He looked straight ahead. Nothing was said. Silence grew thick between them—a separating silence, like a wall of ice.

In the traffic of the streets, with the noise and hurry about them, the strain of their silence lessened. They seemed like people going home, tired from a long evening. Too tired to look or talk to each other. At her door, he bade her good-night in an absent voice and turned down the street.

CHAPTER XI

"The moment is our only eternity."

His words rushed upon her as she opened the door of her room. She slumped on the bed and sat staring at the wall.

Each, in his separate orbit, had traveled centuries to reach that moment. He had left the track of generations of puritan training and burst into this blaze of life. And she, who had longed for the warm intimacy of that other race that had always been locked to her— she, in her blindness, had resisted that which she had roused in him—resisted not only him but also herself. The moment was gone. Could nothing bring it back?

She kept re-enacting the scene, picturing to herself how it might have been. Might it still be? Was it really over? Over?—It had scarcely begun. Every atom of her body waited for morning.

But the man she found in the office—was he the man of the night before? God! The morning light upon him—within him—around him! He who had been so close, so real, had suddenly become distant, strange, and unreal. His face a mask. His voice a monotone.

There were conferences all that day, and for days after. He was suddenly steeped in work. He was writing articles for the magazines, preparing a manuscript for the publisher, attending to long delayed correspondence. Another stenographer was hired to assist the stenographer and he kept them both working overtime.

Once, when she found him alone in his office, she asked: "Will you have a little free time this evening?"

He was embarrassed and pointed to a pile of galleys on his crowded desk.

"This has to be sent to the publisher by tomorrow morning—even if I have to stay up all night to do it."

He caught her looking at him as if, seeing into his thoughts, she had made some ghastly discovery. The look was so uncannily intent that he turned away his eyes. In that instant a curtain seemed suddenly to have been drawn aside and she saw how tired he was. His face had grown thinner, paler, lines, like thieves in the night, creeping stealthily across the forehead. Shadows dulled his eyes. Even his hair had lost its luster.

Dimly, very dimly she glimpsed the disappointment, the disillusion drowned in his business. He had expected from her the passionate warmth, the fullness of feeling of a woman of the people—and how she had failed him! What use had he for her romantic hero-worship? He wanted love. Love in his terms. Love at this moment...

"Have you finished translating the editorial?" he asked, turning his head to the window.

"Oh—uh—that editorial?" She looked at him like one waking from sleep. The editorial was so unimportant. "It's almost ready. I'll have it for you this afternoon."

She managed to get herself out of his office. In her

room she sat before her desk, facing the typewriter with a look of fixed confusion in her eyes.

All at once, like a clap of thunder, her mood changed. She began pacing up and down her room. Her whole body screwed tense.

"I can't stuff myself with work the way he does," the words tumbled out of her in a passion of revolt. "And such work! The big bluff!"

Miss Foster, whose room was below, thrust her head in the door. "Is there anything wrong?" she asked.

"Nothing. Nothing."

Miss Foster reluctantly closed the door.

Fanya turned back to the typewriter. She started to read the editorial, then abruptly pulling out the page, tore it into bits, snatched up the newspaper, threw it into the waste-basket, seized the manuscripts on her desk, destroyed them piece by piece, and without stopping for hat or coat, stormed out of the room.

Hours later, when she returned, the house was in darkness. She crept up to her room and slumped heavily into a chair. Like a creature of stone, she sat by the window, watching the endless night.

Slowly, dim stirrings in the chaos of her mind brought up fragments—disjointed memories. The finding and the losing of him whirled about her in a blinding turmoil of confusion.

How she had rushed to him! One need possessed her. The need for understanding. No other race was ever cursed with such obsession for understanding as hers. Because they were ostracized and exiled and forced to be different from the rest.... She didn't want to be different. She wanted to break through the thing that separated her from his kind....

When she came to him, he saw no difference. He knew her instantly. He gave her herself, her people, her background, her roots, her soil, her inner nourishment. And suddenly—did he get tired of giving? When he reached out—what had she to give him?

In her super-sensitized state, she carried on imaginary conversations with him.

"There's no glory in suffering," he seemed to say to her. "We must get on with our job. Self-pity is our worst vice—an indulgence we cannot allow ourselves. Get to work, Fanya!"

"But what's my work? How can I work without love?"

"There's no time for love, the way you want it."

"No time for love?"

"No time for the personal, possessive love that scatters and wastes our energies. You must put love in its place. An incident—not our whole existence."

"I lost my whole existence in you. You are more my own than my own people. No one knows me as you know me. You can make me live or die with a breath, a turn of an eyelash."

"Hush! Be reasonable. Stop interpreting me in the image you have made of me."

Always his reason would dominate her blind, importunate clamoring. To escape from the dominance of his mind over her, she would cease her fanciful conversations with him to fling her questions to the deaf and dumb air.

"Are his duties only to his work, his family, to the

children of his flesh? Has he no allegiance to the children of his spirit?"

And out of the deaf and dumb air would come her own answer:

"Who are you to make any claims on him? Because in an off moment from his work, he stopped to be kind to you—have you a mortgage on his soul forever?"

Through the days and weeks that followed, he went on working. She went on wasting herself in an agony of inaction—watching the stride of his work.

She saw the pilgrim fathers, the steady, disciplined energy of five generations of Massachusetts farmers back of him—making his days one long integrity of accomplishment. His was the brain of a long line of conquering pioneers—men and women whose life was action—not introspection. They asked for no manna from heaven—no saviour to save them. They set about with cool, clear heads, ordering their lives step by step, mounting from one achievement to another, till they stood unshaken in their own strength—victors over the wilderness. Success was bred into his blood and bone just as defeat was bred into hers.

Was it because he and his ancestors had fought an external wilderness that they could be so triumphant now?

Back of her was a scattered race overcome by forces that they could not get hold of and make their own. Uncertainty, insecurity drove them—where they knew not. Theirs was an internal wilderness as well as the wilderness of the world. A confusion of voices—runaway emotions about which they could not reason and which they could not overcome until they had achieved a philosophy of life. And until then—they could only go about—homeless wanderers—unshepherded sheep of thought lost in trackless wilds of untamed desire.

* * *

They were asked to write their final reports. The investigation was finished.

"I can't write a report," she blurted when she found him alone. "The whole study is as unreal as social work and helping the poor."

"But a good deal of social work is constructive. And helping the poor is a necessary evil until we can abolish poverty."

"You know less about the Poles than when you started out to study them three months ago. Reports only cover the chasm."

There was a swift raising of his eyebrows. His jaws had suddenly become more prominent. "Haven't we had a competent staff of investigators? Haven't we interviewed representative leaders of the community? Haven't we gathered data from a large number of families? Haven't we examined basic social and economic conditions among them?"

"Well, what have we got? Words—words—words. We have been awfully busy—with—with nothing—"

"After all, a report is only a record of what we attempted to do. It seems little enough. Yet as in all sciences, a little straw here and a little straw there tells which way the wind blows."

"You know nothing about the *heart* of the Poles. Without love, what is there to write about?"

"Don't be ridiculous. You are confusing things hopelessly. You are unable to see beyond the one emotion of yours that has no application to this work which we have on hand. We are not talking in terms of love and passion, both of which are products of the individual. We are talking in terms of groups and we're dealing with them with our intelligence. How far do you think the human race would go if everyone did nothing but feel? We are fortunately endowed with brains that permit us to co-ordinate results of our feelings and impressions and even move in the realm of pure reason. Your wild gesture is only a defense of your unwillingness to concentrate and organize your thoughts."

She sat staring at the floor. Something in her face suddenly moved him. He passed his hand over his forehead and bent toward her. "Fanya, aren't you being a bit hysterical today? Problems are solved by reason—not emotion. You are ardent and emotional, and your approach is always a personal one; but unfortunately it won't do in a case like this. Try to leave yourself out of it for once—if a woman ever could—"

"You can be so cold, so impersonal because you can shut out your heart the way some people shut off a room they don't want to use. Reason! It's always reason with you! What has reason got to do with it? I've been to you only a mood—a moment. And so—And so—

"Emotion—I'm tired of it." He walked over to his bookcase and took out books and put them back again.

She nodded her head drearily. She was beaten. She was as helpless as a child in a futile conflict with a grown-up whose will was law. She was miserably and humiliatingly in love with this man who no longer loved her. The shame and the hurt of it would go on gnawing and burning to the end of her days.

She saw him stir uneasily and glance at the clock.

"I might as well give it up," she said, in a very low voice. "This research is for professors and doctors of philosophy.... Your understanding—it was only a dream. You can't understand with the mind. You've got to live our lives to feel us with the heart. What do you know of suffering as we know it? A tiny pang—a poem—and you can pass on to your philosophy. Your feelings do not have to go through flesh and blood. You catch a breath of them—and your mind builds up the rest with words and formulas."

He sat up straight in his chair and put the distance of a polite smile between them.

His smile was like oil on flames.

"You're not big enough to face failure," she hurled at him. "What you don't know—what you don't understand you cover up with words. It's a blasphemy of God in people to carry on studies in that spirit. The beauty, the madness, the pain, and the grandeur that make up the song of life—all the hidden things that can't be put into words—are lost to you."

"What you are saying has nothing to do with this report. You've got an attack of nerves and are not in a fit state to do anything."

The scene had gone on too long. In another minute

she would be weeping and repel him still more because
she was what she was. With a sudden lift of her head,
she rose and walked out strangely straight and silent.

PART II

CHAPTER XII

The Great Hall, set for the banquet, floated before her in a sort of dazzling confusion. It all seemed so blurred and unreal to Fanya lvanowna, standing there in the receiving line, between the president of the university and the president of the graduate journalistic society. The lights, the flowers, the music, and the whirl of faces straining toward her. The line was endless. Six hundred hands to shake. Six hundred college men and women, with their curious, sensation-seeking eyes, imprisoning her in their appraisal, till she felt like a puppet in a play.

They had invited her to speak to them about herself. They wanted the story of poverty they had read about in her novels. The sweatshop of New York where she had sewed buttons on shirts from early morning till late at night, for three dollars a week. The crowded tenement where she had lived with twelve others in one room and fared on cabbage soup and black bread. Nothing about that lurid slum life was too sordid for them to hear. The sordidness thrilled them because it had led to success.

A sense of exile and loneliness swept over her in the midst of the flattering, friendly phrases as they shook hands. What a bluff she was—standing there, flushed and smiling—their symbol of success! If they could look into her heart and see the darkness in which she was plunged, even here in the center of the spotlight.

She had come quite unwillingly. When they had written to her, she had answered promptly that she wasn't a speaker. Then the president of the society telephoned and insisted that they must have her.

"But I'm not a lecturer," she protested. "You'd be so disappointed."

"Not at all. We want to see you."

At that, Fanya named a forbidding fee to put an end to the matter. But her high price only enhanced her importance to these success-seekers. She had to come.

"But what can I talk about?"

"Your life. Your life is so interesting. Tell us what made you a writer."

As though it were as simple as all that. As though she could assemble the scattered bits of her experience that was her life and serve it to them from the platform like a social cup of tea.

What would they say if she could tell them quite simply that her success was born of bitterest failure— the failure to hold a great friendship, a great love.

The failure to accept his phenomenal kindness of ten years ago— In spite of her bungling at the research study, he had still tried to help her find herself in work. He had recommended her to a settlement, to the Immigrant Aid Society, to the Association for Helping the Poor. Why had she failed to respond to such generous interest? She was too proud to accept kindness when love had ceased? Or was it her unreasonable aversion to social work? Perhaps the very work he had suggested made her see how far apart were the worlds in which they lived. Trying to recapture the vanished dream, that had for a moment brought them together, forced her to write. Through her writing, she still hoped to reach him who had gone beyond reach. This and a lot more that she could not even phrase to herself was in her mind.

But at dinner, when she looked into the expectant faces of her audience, she felt old. They were like little children eagerly awaiting a fairy-tale. They had come to hear it. Why disappoint them? So she told them the story newspapers had featured in headlines—"From Rags to Riches"—"From the Sweatshop to Society."

"I had been writing and starving for years," she began. "My novel, *Alien Souls,* although praised by reviewers, had brought me little money and almost no recognition. People who read a book little know of the small reward there is for the writer while he is unknown—of his often solitary, starved existence.

"My poverty had reached the breaking point. My rent was overdue, and the landlady had put out my belongings on the sidewalk, in the rain. My only possessions, a typewriter, a box of manuscripts, a dictionary, and a few books of poetry were ruined and I was too desperate to care.

"I walked the streets for days. My only food crusts of bread picked out of garbage cans." She paused dramatically to note the little shudder that rose to her from the audience.

"Suicide seemed the only logical end to my misery. But before taking my life, I felt I had to have a talk with the editor of the publishing house. He had often told me that before long one of my books would 'go over big' and I would be famous. He had told me there was a grim humor in all my stories. My tragic characters were all funny people who made him laugh. And I had decided to go to him and ask which would be funnier, to jump off some skyscraper or fling myself down from Brooklyn Bridge.

"But when I was shown into his office, before I had a chance to open my lips, he exclaimed, 'Why, I've been expecting you for the last two days.'

"'Expecting me?'

"'Didn't you get my telegram?'

"I stared at him. 'More of his humor,' I thought bitterly.

"'Great news!' He smiled into my sullen face. 'Woman, you're made!'

"'What are you talking about?'

"'Two motion picture companies are bidding for your novel. All you've got to do is sign. Now—what did I tell you?'

"The world changed and I was changed.

"After the negotiations for the book had been completed, the company offered to send me to California to collaborate on the screen version of *Alien Souls*.

"Arrived in Los Angeles, I was greeted with overwhelming friendliness by the representative of the company. Then I was driven to one of the best hotels. Flowers filled my room. Luxurious comforts beyond dreams all about me. With the push of a button, maids and bellboys ready to wait on me. I felt dazzled out of my senses with this sudden plunge into the world of wealth.

"That evening, I attended the first dinner of 'The Eminent Authors.'

"Cocktails were served as we seated ourselves about the table. A millionaire's feast was spread before my eyes. Four butlers busy serving a dozen guests. Champagne—it would be impossible to count the bottles. As one rich dish after another was served, I thought of that cold, winter night, not so long ago, when I stood with the bums and outcasts of the earth in the Bowery bread line, shivering for hours, for a cup of coffee and a slice of bread. I had touched the two extremes of life—the Bowery bread line—the feasting of Hollywood."

The audience listened, awed, breathless as Fanya reached the climax of her story.

"At my right hand sat Will Rogers, and all about us, authors and czars of the movies—East Side boys who had risen from cloak and suit factories, and now had power to buy up American authors and all their works. Will Rogers, the clown prince, poked fun at them all. I saw how funny he was, but I could not laugh below my head. I felt like the outside child at the party. I could only watch the game, but I didn't know how to play.

"Suddenly, the wise jester, who had amused kings and queens and presidents of the two continents, swung around, leaned his quizzical, laughter-crinkled face close to mine.

"'Say—Alien Soul, don't you ever laugh? What's your grouch? Aren't you in the Movies? What are you thinking of, looking on with those alien eyes of yours?'

"'I've been thinking that the cost of champagne for this one dinner would be enough to buy milk for a whole block of starving tenement children for a month.'"

Applause filled the banquet hall when Fanya sat down. The clapping of hands and stamping of feet went on and on, like some tumultuous music.

"Poor, foolish sheep!" Fanya thought, as they crowded around, gushing gratitude for her "inspired talk" and besieging her with invitations to stay.

On her way back home, that night, in the Pullman compartment, she could not sleep. Excitement had keyed up her nerves to such a pitch. A sense of failure, of guilt, roused her from her fatigue.

Peering out of her window into the dark, she saw again the eager faces of the men and women who had come to hear her speak. Why had she cheated them with the gilt and glitter of her Hollywood success? What things she might have told them far more dramatic than her experience in Hollywood, if she had had more faith in herself and more faith in them!

The door of American prosperity had opened for her. She had stepped through that door, only to drop back to her isolation. There was no glamour, no illusion for her in the turn of fortune that made her society's puppy for the moment. Surfeited with teas, lunches, dinners. And yet the wolf was still at her door. The wolf in a different guise.

CHAPTER XIII

One morning, a few days after the banquet, Fanya looked about her beautiful studio. Air, sunshine, quiet—everything needed for comfort was here. More than comfort. This clean, lonely silence, this spacious emptiness was the workshop she had longed for when she was poor. But slowly, as year gave way to year, the peace and luxury that had left her so free to create had turned into a prison—an island of sterile emptiness.

Aside from the barrenness of accomplishment in this now barren setting, the air was thick with thought of him whom she had tried to forget. There was the couch where she had been lying awake nights, struggling to free herself from the thought of him. The chair, the fireplace before which she had, for hours upon hours, wrestled with memories. The very typewriter was weighted with countless attempts to pluck him out of her heart in words—only to fail.

She went and looked at herself in the mirror. This was the face and body she had to live with day by day—the image of herself she longed to be rid of, because it stood between her and her work, impalpable and menacing. She examined herself critically, with a detachment that was the thin, cold edge of despair;

her face—tired and lined and white, the face of a woman who has come to middle age before her time; her body, splendid and vital; body betraying face and face betraying body.

With her mind she denied love—except the bitter memory of it, and that she would have denied if she could; but her body had ripened for it year by year, against her will; and today this discrepancy seemed more than ever grotesque.

When men looked at her in the streets, or met her for the first time, she thought she detected a mixture of admiration and insolence and pity in their eyes. And because of this, the burden of her ruined love became more intolerable every day.

Perhaps, she thought, if she walked out of this place, stripped of everything; if she gave up the bath, the steam heat, and the three meals a day; if she started again in the shop, the factory, anywhere where there was common work among common people; she might learn to forget him, and to live again.

A complete change was necessary to break the deadlock of her wasted days.

Fanya glanced at her watch. Eight o'clock. She usually had her coffee at six. She had never outgrown her old-time factory habit of rising at five in the morning. It was like an alarm clock in her body that shook her out of sleep no matter how late she went to bed. For all her ten years in the Village, she could never learn its artistic habit of staying in bed until noon.

While at breakfast she glanced at the headlines of the newspaper. Then she deliberately turned to the

"Help Wanted" columns. Why not make the break now—at once?

"HANDS FOR KNITTING MACHINES!" That sounded humble enough. She left the breakfast dishes unwashed, picked up her hat and purse and started out in her hunt for a job.

What a relief to give up the false life of fictionalizing her experiences—turning herself inside out into words. This unnatural wearing out of body and brain, forcing people out of air. Forever driven with a thought here and a feeling there to make something out of nothing. Once and for all she must end "this fiery trial of untruth," in some honest work—a hand among hands.

Already she saw a picture of herself as "one of them" in the factory. The twelve o'clock whistle. Men and women jumping up from their machines with shouts of joy—starving animals rushing for food. The crowding about the steaming cauldron of tea—each pushing and elbowing the other to be first to fill his cup with something hot. The old apple-woman with her basket of apples, pretzels, pickles, and penny-pieces of herring, hawking her wares. Groups sitting about on their machines, on the windowsills, laughing and talking as they opened their newspaper bundles of lunch. The smell of onions, pickles, and herring rioting in the air.

Now she'd love all she had once hated. The smells, the shrill voices, the unwashed necks that used to make her so ill. There was something unwashed, something shrill in her own soul that Henry Scott had rejected. And she, the rejected one, must henceforth take to her heart all the despised and rejected of the earth.

Already she felt the refreshing contact of her own people. Already she had strength enough to tear herself free from the need of him. Instead of wasting herself any more in hopeless longing for the man who didn't want her, she'd serve her own people. They who hungered and thirsted and suffered as she had—they needed her. To them she would give the understanding she longed for but never could have for herself.

She saw herself shouldering their fight for higher wages, educating them to demand better working conditions—light—air—recreation rooms. But at the factory door a brick mountain of gloom rose over her. Through the grated windows the whirr and thunder of deafening machines...

Are you lying to yourself again? Lose yourself in this hell of noise? Glorify your soul's confusion as a Hand among Hands? Can you who have once escaped from all this go back? Can you be an immigrant twice in a lifetime?...

She raced up the steps to beat the pursuing voices. Damn this introspection!

Boldly she pushed herself into the line of waiting applicants. Young girls with all shades of rouge on their cheeks, high heels, smart gaudy styles, before and behind her. Her pale, natural skin looked sickly against their high-colored faces. The very simplicity of her clothes betrayed her difference from them.

She suddenly became aware of her age against their youth. None of them was more than sixteen, eighteen, or at the most twenty years. I am so much older, she thought, so much older—and yet with less worldly sense than any of these young things. Thirty-three years old and still a lost adolescent,—fleeing,—fleeing from what?

"Next," came from the thick-lipped boss. His suspicious glance took her in, from her plain felt hat to her low-heeled shoes.

"What do you want here?" he said accusingly.

"About the ad," she stammered.

"Well, what about it? Who sent you? The Union, or the Board of Health?"

"Oh, no. I came for a job."

"I'm no greenhorn," he sneered, the little spiteful mouth tight and hard as the gold of his front teeth. "I want no ladies snooping around my shop."

"I'm no lady. If I were a lady, would I apply to you for work? I tell you I want work."

"And I tell you I want *Hands*, not *Heads*. Next."

She made one last effort to fight his rejection.

"What do you have against me?" she demanded.

"You look too pale and you talk too smart."

She had raced up with impulsive haste. Slowly, thoughtfully she picked her way down the stairs.... He with his thick lips, his thick neck, saw through my lie. I've not been sincere even with myself. I've got to be truthful. But what is the truth...? Perhaps he's right. I don't belong there. Other places where I could fit in better and still touch the roots of life.

A whole morning gone. She had been rejected, but she had come a shade nearer the truth, whatever the truth was. Though she was very tired, she was not wholly discouraged. She decided to apply to Craft's. They had advertised for chocolate dippers.

The way to the office led through the shopping district of Fifth Avenue. Throngs of people wound their way up and down the sidewalks. Fanya watched their tense, busy faces, as they hurried in and out of stores, darting desirous eyes at shop windows. How busy they all were! Busy with what? Buying and buying. Another hat, another gown, a marcel, a facial. Anyway they were busy with things that carried them on. On—away from themselves. The commonplace nothings of everyday kept them going. The movie, the theatre, dressing up, eating and talking saved them from thought.

A shop girl in a tawdry velvet dress, a hat with a bright brass buckle in front, holding in her hand a crumpled page of "Want Ads," paused before the window of Maurice Chapelle, gazed longingly at a soft, satin negligee with trailing, filmy sleeves of Viennese lace. It was as though a mirror had suddenly been held up to Fanya's eyes. Her compassion for the deluded shop girl brought her face to face with her own absurdity.

Smiling ruefully, she walked into Craft's employment office.

Miss Stillman, the efficient employment manager, was as different from the thick-lipped, thick-necked boss as her office was different from the dirty noisy knitting factory. Fanya caught a glimpse of the woman through the open door of the waiting room. What kind intelligence smiled in that face! That look of confident common sense. The coolness of a person who was master of life. Wasn't she a little too cool? A little too much master?

As she entered the office, Fanya decided she would be absolutely sincere. Here was a woman intelligent enough to understand, someone to whom she must tell the truth about herself.

Miss Stillman's friendly, "How do you do?" was all that Fanya needed to open her heart. She spoke eagerly.

"I'm anxious to find work—any work."

"What have you been doing? "

"Nothing much—just writing."

"M'm! Writing?" Miss Stillman regarded the applicant with a dubious smile. The old-fashioned hat. The eyes far off—lost in herself.

And then Fanya saw the repulsion that this coldly efficient, coldly sympathetic woman felt for her. Miss Stillman had perceived, had wanted to perceive, no more than what was on the surface. Fanya's physical magnetism she felt—but it disgusted her; to Miss Stillman no woman who looked so middle-aged, so tired, should have a body that could speak as Fanya's spoke. It was almost indecent: or, what was worse, unreasonable. "You're a poet, I suppose?"

"A poet?" Fanya answered, trying to keep the weariness from her voice. "Not exactly. I've written some half dozen books—novels and short stories."

"Then why do you want a job at Craft's?"

"I've suffered a terrible disillusion—a loss of faith that left me in utter darkness. All I want now is a job to keep busy, to stop the agony of thoughts that can't come through."

At the intensity in Fanya's voice, the flame in her eyes, Miss Stillman's feet stiffened. Accustomed as she was to all sorts of people, this was too much. Her hand involuntarily moved across the desk toward the emergency button.

"All I want is a chance to forget myself in busy work—anything to be among people again."

In her impulsive ardor, Fanya started from her chair to impress her plea upon Miss Stillman. Down went the finger on the emergency button.

Two husky matrons appeared like magic at the door. Assured of her body-guard, Miss Stillman brushed aside the ghetto-bottled vehemence and began her questionnaire.

"What is your name?"

"Fanya lvanowna."

A shadow of relief passed over Miss Stillman's eyes. Her face relaxed in an amused smile. "Fanya lvanowna is the name of an author."

"I am Fanya Ivanowna." She showed Miss Stillman a publisher's letter asking when they could count on her next novel, a letter she had received the day before.

"Oh, so you're only a harmless author?" Then with a certain degree of deference, "I've read reviews of your books, and something you wrote once in the *Atlantic Monthly*." In a gracious apologetic tone, she added, "You know, all sorts of queer people come looking for jobs here."

With a nod, she dismissed the matrons, and turned back to Fanya.

"So you're looking for new material for your next novel?"

"Oh, no. Something has stopped the writing in me." She pressed her tense hands together. "I don't believe

I shall ever write again unless I can get back to the real life I once lived when I worked in the factory."

"But you've made a name for yourself as an author. Would you give up fame for—?"

"Fame is a more terrible trap than love. Is there anything as treacherous as the applause of the mob?"

Fanya passed her hands tensely along her lap. "It's because I want again the peace of obscurity that I've come to you for a job. Dipping chocolates, wrapping candy, any dead grind, only to stop the pain of thought and feeling that eats out my heart. I'm more in need of something to do than when I was merely working for bread. I've got to work to save my soul."

The half-amused smile returned to Miss Stillman's lips.

"But Craft's are not in business to save souls. They're in business to make candy. We are like one happy family here. I'm afraid you wouldn't fit in. Don't you see?"

Fanya's inward-gazing eyes, diverted for a moment from their introspection, saw Miss Stillman, now business-like, cold, efficient.

"Why? Why wouldn't I fit into your happy family?"

"Because your chief interest is writing, not the making of candy. You don't want work. You want atmosphere. I'm sorry. If it depended on me ... But my job is to hire workers, not authors. I'm afraid Craft's doesn't want people around with unwritten stories buzzing in their brains."

"I'd be willing to work without money till I prove to you my worth."

Miss Stillman did not answer. She examined the pencil in her hand.

"All I ask is a chance. If you would only try me."

Miss Stillman glanced at the clock, then at Fanya across the big desk.

"I am willing to work. Haven't I the right to work?"

Miss Stillman was still sizing her up. Sizing her up with her distant gaze.

"You might as well say that a blind man has a right to see, or a lame man a right to walk—"

"You mean to say that an author who wants a job is like a blind man trying to see or a lame man trying to walk?"

"Perhaps," came in a cool, precise voice, smiling kindly.

Fanya's hand went over her eyes as though to ward off a blow. "Why? Why?" she implored.

"How old are you?" Miss Stillman's sharp eyes traveled over Fanya's tired face, the greying hair, the sagging lines of her neck. Fanya sat very still, eyes fixed on nothing.

"Thirty-three," she said, looking toward Miss Stillman but not at her.

"Twenty-five years is the age limit at Craft's."

"You mean to say I'm too old? Why—I feel younger than youth in spirit."

"What you feel in spirit may be of use in your art. But factories do not want brains and spirit. They want brawn, muscle. With us over thirty is the deadline."

"You condemn me to the deadline? "

Miss Stillman gave a low, little laugh. "A firebrand

like you—let loose among our employees! All the established discipline of the factory would go by the board."

"Oh-h-h! So that is what you think of me? I—a firebrand?"

"Really, Miss Ivanowna," she said with amused tolerance, "if you could only stop long enough to *know yourself,* you'd see how unreasonable ... "

"What is there unreasonable in my cry for work? You say because I've been found guilty of authorship, I'm not fit for honest work?"

The smile went out of Miss Stillman's eyes. Her brows contracted into hard, unrelenting lines but her voice remained low and self-controlled.

"You writers are so conceited! You think because you can write, you can do anything you want to. You claim your right to work. Would you deny me the equal right to choose whom to employ? Certain psychologists claim it would be a good thing for one's individual development to change occupations every few years. But at whose expense is such individual development to be? Suppose I should find myself out of a job in my own profession and should want to turn author—who'd care to buy my books?"

Fanya listened with wide, earnest eyes, carried away by the force of the arguments arrayed against her. "I am beginning to see your side of it more clearly than my own," she confessed. "But what shall I do? I must find a job."

"My dear," Miss Stillman put a kind hand on her shoulder, as they walked to the door, "Craft's is not the place for you. You'd never be happy with us. There is a right place for you, as there is a right place for all of us."

Fanya smiled in spite of her dejection, as the door closed behind her. "What's my right place?"

Henry's quick understanding flashed like lightning against the merciless judgment of the efficiency expert. The clamor of the street, the crowds passing by, the air, the sky filled her with the conquering force that he unbound....

> "All I could never be,
> All, men ignored in me,
> That I was worth to God...."*

It was already dusk in the deep shadowed streets when she got back to her studio. She fixed a tray of food and brought it to her worktable at the window. The walls of the room seemed to dissolve in the dusk. The boat horns called mournfully from the river. The faint notes of a piano, "Pelléas and Mélisande," drifted in from somewhere nearby. But the room itself was very quiet.

As she ate, she saw the dark hall-room of the tenement in which Henry had once come to see her. From darkness, from hunger, he had delivered her with the magic of a look. She felt very young. Almost gay.

She got up from the table and walked over to the mirror hanging opposite the window. In its calm

---

*Ed. note: Yezierksa has slightly misquoted Robert Browning here, as the third line actually reads, "This, I was worth to God...." She has also inaccurately reproduced the alignment. The editors have decided to remain as faithful as possible to Yezierska's original text. For the correct poem excerpt, see page one, the half-title page in this edition.

depths she saw the smoky blue outlines of the twilight city. Against buildings merged with the dim haze, she saw her own face, touched with twilight, bright with the remembrance of his love.

She smiled shyly at herself.

"Fanya! Fanya!" she breathed, softly, feigning his voice. She had caught again that sense of her own brightness, of something special and rare in herself that he had always been able to give her. She bent toward the image of herself in the mirror as if to touch it with her lips.

"Thirty years! The deadline!" Miss Stillman's cool voice, her look of appraisal crashed in upon her. "Thirty years!" she repeated. Henry knew her ten years ago.

Wearily, she snapped on the light above the mirror. Thirty-three years looked back at her.

CHAPTER XIV

To get the chill of Miss Stillman's cold appraisal out of her bones, Fanya thought of Helena Hoffman, the librarian. Miss Hoffman—warm, reassuring—eyes strangely young under the greying hair. Time went on bringing discouragement, hopelessness, indifference, and physical changes to others; but Helena Hoffman possessed a tranquility of spirit that kept her above the wear and tear of the years. A woman in her fifties—and yet her face still held the light of youth—an untiring capacity for living and doing.

Years ago, Fanya used to come to Miss Hoffman's library to keep warm and escape from the shrieking noises of the tenement where she had to live. And now, as she approached the building, the tension, the merciless fight with the world dropped away. It was like coming upon sanctuary. There was an air of enduring peace about the place. The pictures, the shelves of books waiting for their readers.

Here it was cool in summer, warm in winter. People felt free to come and rest and think as long as they liked, reading, or pretending to read.

Though it was a branch of the public library, everybody referred to it as "Miss Hoffman's library." She had been librarian there so many years, she had become part of the library, or the library had become part of her.

The place ran loosely, without any of the red tape of a city institution. Was it Helena Hoffman who had made a social center, a clubhouse out of the library, or had the people of the neighborhood taken possession of the place and run it as if it were their own? Nobody cared. It lived without laws. Every week there was something new going on—an exhibit, a song recital, a folk dance, a talk on some timely topic. But whatever went on—Helena Hoffman was the hub of the wheel around which it all revolved.

Painters, writers brought their work to her for criticism. If anyone had a spark in them, Helena Hoffman had the gift for making much of it. She found a young photographer doing original things and she invited him to show his work. An old gentlewoman who had lost her fortune was trying to make a living selling embroideries and patchwork quilts. Miss Hoffman arranged an exhibit of her wares. It seemed to Fanya that just talking to Miss Hoffman would break through her inability to get a job.

She was busy at the front desk. A line of people were waiting to have their books stamped. Fanya took her place at the end of the line, but Miss Hoffman, catching sight of her, turned the details over to her assistant and came straight to Fanya.

"What have you been doing with yourself?" She greeted her with outstretched hands. "I was on the point of writing or phoning you to come to the opening of the library roof-garden next Sunday. If I announce that Fanya Ivanowna will come, there will be a crowd, rain or shine."

Fanya smiled ruefully.

"You must see how down and out I feel or you wouldn't put it on so thick."

Miss Hoffman gave her an affectionate shove. "What you need is a little more conceit. A certain amount of humility is good for the soul, but you've allowed humility to become a vice."

A mist filled Fanya's eyes as she looked at her friend. One minute she praised; the next minute she scolded, but always the one thing that mattered to Helena Hoffman was her welfare. Courage, confidence began to flow in Fanya's heart again.

"Some librarians are interested only in the books on the shelves. With you, it's people—"

"You are not just people," said Miss Hoffman, smoothing back a stray lock of Fanya's hair. "You belong to me. I watched you start your career. I look for so much in you."

Miss Hoffman led Fanya to her office. As she took her seat opposite her friend, Fanya felt like a little chick, crawling under the shelter of its mother's wing.

"I've just been told that I belong to the deadline," Fanya blurted and she related her interview with Miss Stillman.

"People have such a romantic notion of what an author should be that when you want to do ordinary work, you become a double failure in their eyes," said Miss Hoffman. "If you are in earnest about giving your writing a rest and taking a job, you must invent a ready-made story that will make you credible to the employer."

She picked up a newspaper, scanned the advertisements. "Look. So many stores want salesladies."

Fanya glanced at the page. "I'll go tomorrow. In a department store you meet all kinds of people."

Miss Hoffman tapped with a pencil on Fanya's shapeless hat. "Child! You have no chance at all with this lid."

"I know. A day's shopping is before me. The mere thought of it—" Fanya's whole body sagged under the burden. "The hardest part of getting a job is dressing up for it. Isn't it ridiculous to have to rouge and doll up in new clothes when inside I feel old and dead enough to have grass grow over me?"

Miss Hoffman put her hand strongly about Fanya's waist. "Come,"—she laughed with a faint note of mockery in her voice—"the play has to go on no matter how the actors feel. Let me show you the roof-garden ready for the opening."

Fanya followed silently. They sat down on a wicker bench, ferns and flowers all about them. Slowly, the peace of the sky worked its spell.

In the moonlight, Helena Hoffman's face was like the face of some priestess who had learned the secret of serenity from the gods.

There was a story current among the friends of Miss Hoffman's youth. Something about a younger sister to whom she had given both her wedding gown and her fiancé.

To this day the story was kept alive by the dressmaker, now a tottering, old woman who had been called in to refit the dress for the younger sister. How much truth, how much fiction there was in what was being said, Fanya did not know, but the story fitted Helena Hoffman like the shadows about her eyes.

"Whenever I get too tense about life," said Miss Hoffman, "I come here and look at the stars."

"I used to hate the coldness, the peace of the stars," Fanya thought aloud. "I wanted life, action—not far-off things. Now I begin to get a dim idea of their meaning."

Silence hushed the very breath of thought. Miss Stillman, Henry, her little self, and all her little dreams and desires dropped away. What was the world and all the people in it, but a speck of dust in the vast immensity of this outer universe?

She looked at Helena Hoffman sitting so quietly under the stars and the echo of well-known words sounded in her ears—*"When I consider Thy Heavens . . . What is man that Thou art mindful of him?"* . . . An ancient, comforting picture arose before her: King David on the roof of the temple communing with God while the child lay sleeping at his feet.

CHAPTER XV

The next morning brought her back to the treadmill of hurry, the sordid realities of her unreal days. A job. Clothes. She had to start the round of the stores, hunting for a new outfit.

The first day of shopping was agony. Not a dress, not a hat that she tried on seemed to fit her. She felt like a scarecrow in the ready-mades cut by the gross. Going from one Tower of Babel to another. Clothes—clothes—a million rows of all kinds of dresses, hats, coats—and nothing just right for her.

In despair, she decided to try one of the more expensive shops on Fifty-seventh Street. What a huge waste of time and energy it was to try to make an appearance, she thought, on her way to Milgrim's.

A Jack London could come to the most formal evening affair in a blue woolen shirt and have all the evening gowns and full dress suits bow down to him. Do homage even to the blue woolen shirt he happened to wear. That was the glory of being an artist. Every bit of your nonconformity added to your power. Everything against you in ordinary life worked for you as an artist. As long as she could produce, no one noticed the sallow complexion, the tired strain of sleeplessness. Then she had power to make the world take her at her own valuation.

At the entrance of Milgrim's, she paused. The stolid, ox-eyed flunkey in his green uniform with the brass buttons, the smart clothes in the show window, the air of materialism exuding out on the sidewalk scattered her thoughts.

In a state of reluctant bewilderment, she felt herself drawn into an atmosphere of beauty and sophistication, drugged under the spell of it, as if she had tasted some strange opiate that had transformed her into a new being. Here was wealth dissolved in melodies of color and line. Hangings, carpets, walls—blending chords of music.

Her feet sank into a soft, velvet-padded rug, as she walked up the steps to the throne room. "The throne of Mammon—the throne of vanity and illusion," a faint voice whispered within her. She walked on. A stately, queenlike woman approaching, roused her from her trance.

Fanya became aware of her shabby blue serge, the holes in her gloves, the straggling hair—All her imperfections leaped at her at sight of this immaculately groomed saleswoman.

"What can I do for you, Madam?" The woman sized her up with her questioning smile.

"Have you a gown like the one you are wearing?"

"Why, we never duplicate our models. But I'll show you our latest importations."

Fanya was led through the spacious throne room to a small salon in warm, wine-colored velvet. The woman pointed to a damask chair and vanished. Through the open door, Fanya saw other grey-haired fashion queens, and their young, panther-like mani-kins, displaying with sophisticated ease the last word in style.

The dazzling elegance of these saleswomen! What poise, what power they possessed—or seemed to pos-sess just because they were perfectly gowned. Most of them long past forty. But were they in the deadline? Their studied grace, their art made youth feel awk-ward—old. Rouge, lipstick, mascara—used as they used them—were as fine an art as painting.... Job-hunting was war.... Clothes and all the hidden little arts that made for appearance were the implements of this war.... She would equip herself for battle this time, even if she had to plunge all her savings to do it.

The woman returned with an armful of dresses.

"Too stylish! Too Frenchy!" Fanya shook her head in disapproval as she held up one frock after another.

Suddenly, she saw on the chair a superlatively sim-ple black satin that the woman had overlooked.

"This is what I want!" Fanya cried, snatching it up.

She tried it on. Before she saw herself in the mirror, she knew by the very feel of it, it was for her. This was style, simplicity and, strange to say, this was herself.

Why, she thought to herself in wonder—she loved clothes. She loved satin and always made herself believe that she had preferred serge. She had been like those old maids who say they hate men because men have passed them by.

"How much?" Fanya asked in happy excitement.

"One hundred and sixty dollars," came the cool answer.

One hundred and sixty dollars! That could buy a dozen dresses. But she was too drunk with her rejuvenated appearance to think of cost.

"I'll take it," she heard herself say.

She simply could not tear her eyes away from the mirror. This new vision of herself—in the process of being born. What power in a few yards of material when touched by an artist! The soft sensuous feel of the satin, outlining her body, roused in her a hidden thirst for more and more beauty. The gown that revealed her figure, mocked at her shoes and stockings. Everything had to harmonize with the rhythm of the gown. No wonder women for ages past have sold themselves for clothes! To a real woman, nothing mattered but to be beautiful. Keats knew when he said that beauty was truth.

"Here's a little black felt hat, to complete your costume," said the oracle of style, drawing it down over Fanya's thick auburn hair. It seemed molded on her head just as the satin seemed molded on her figure. This new costume meant a new lease of life, a new courage, a new youth. She had to have it—even if she went bankrupt for it.

"The address, please?" the woman asked.

"Oh, no. I don't want them sent. I'll take them with me." And then realizing she had no money, "I'll be right back. I'm just going to the bank for the amount."

As Fanya turned, she caught, in the triple mirror the impact of an appraising glance. A lady in ermine was arching penciled eyebrows, raising her nose ever so slightly, looking at the decorous saleslady, as if to say,

"What's Hester Street doing on Fifth Avenue?" Fanya flushed, thrust back a hard glare at the white-furred lady—and then wheeled about and walked out....

In less than an hour, she was back, taking the money out of her shabby purse and handing it to the saleslady. She clutched the boxes and departed, too gloriously happy in the new creation of herself to see the puzzled, half-contemptuous smile that followed her.

With the packages in her hand, she went to another shop, bought shoes, chiffon hose, gloves, handkerchiefs, a handbag, lipstick, powder, rouge, creams— she forgot nothing in her drunken orgy of buying.

Next morning Fanya stood before the mirror, marveling at the new person created by a few wisps of chiffon and a few yards of satin. Gazing at this sophisticated transformation of herself, she decided suddenly to change her name. Fanya... Fannie... Fannie something...

Eight o'clock tolled from the Metropolitan Tower, and Fannie Frank started out to look for work. On the top of the world in her new clothes, she was eager to face the most hard-boiled employer.

Tracy's headed the list of stores she was going to try. But when she got there, she found the place jammed with women and girls—all waiting for the same few jobs. So she made for Galchrist's. They too had advertised.

With the studied quiet, the assured step she had just acquired, she walked into the employment office.

"I came in answer to your ad," she said, handing her card to the man at the desk.

At sight of his tailor-made perfection, she rejoiced that she had taken all the time and trouble to put up a front as flawless as his. Now all she needed was to keep cool. Use her head. This was a game. Give him what he wants. Talk his language. Facts. Facts he can tabulate and pigeonhole like the files on his desk.

How thrilling it felt to be so cold in the heart and clear in the head while talking to a man. But was it a man—this smooth-shaven, shrewd-eyed tailor-made model of efficiency?

"Mrs. Frank, have you had any experience?" he looked up at her as he read her card: and from the way he looked, she knew at once that she pleased him. "I've practically been raised in a department store," she smiled down at him." My school, my entire education I got selling goods. Try me out in any line."

"Where did you work last? "

"My last place? Oh—Marshall Field's—in Chicago. I started out as a cash girl. Then worked in the wrapping department. I sold notions in the basement. Then on, from one department to another till I became next to the head of stock in cloaks and suits." Her brain was whirling lies like a spinning top. This was selling fiction instead of writing it. She thought swiftly: This is how criminals begin. They have an imagination that they cannot organize creatively. And so they're driven from lies to crime.

"Why did you leave Marshall Field's?"

"Leave? I did not exactly leave Marshall Field's. But after being in one place ten years, I felt I needed a change. So I decided to come to New York."

"Have you any letters with you?"

A moment of blinding terror she hid under a laugh. "Yes—certainly—I can get you letters—plenty of that sort of thing—any time. I thought it stupid to bring recommendations with me. It's more fun to put yourself over on your own."

The man glanced at her sidewise, smiled, and said nothing. She felt her eyes widening and a special kind of brightness go into them. Her lies gave her a queer heady feeling like one reckless from too much wine.

She leaned forward confidentially, "You know, I hardly wanted to tell you about my experience at Marshall Field's. I want to start in a new place at the beginning."

There was a swift raising of his eyebrows as he looked at her. "Well, well! That's the spirit we need in our store."

He picked up a printed card from his desk. "Here's a little motto I chose for our employees."

Fanya read:

> THE WAY TO SUCCESS:
> 1. Please your employer.
> 2. Co-operate with your fellow-worker.
> 3. Give your best to your job.

"Do you like it?" he asked, enormously pleased with himself.

Fanya looked at him deeply and smiled. "How inspiring it must be to work for you."

Beaming down at her, he handed her an application blank.

"Please fill this out."

As she started to fill out her application, she noticed a square outlined in red:

SECTION 570, PENAL CODE. LAWS OF NEW YORK.
A person who obtains employment or appointment to any office, or place of trust, by color or aid of any false or forged letters, or certificate of recommendation or of any false statement in writing as to his or her name, residence, previous employment or qualification, is guilty of misdemeanor punishable by imprisonment from one day to one year and a fine of $500.00 or both.

Deliberately, she wrote out her new name, Fannie Frank. Then came the account of her experiences at Marshall Field's.

"Everything is fair in love and war," she told herself. "It's war to get a job. If I can't get it telling the truth, I'll tell lies. The end I seek is honest. I only want to live."

When she filled out her application, she brought it to the man. "Are you ready to begin at once?" he asked glancing through it. She nodded.

"I'll take you to our Miss Porter, in charge of new employees." He opened the door and waited for her to pass in.

"Miss Porter, I brought you a new recruit, Mrs. Frank."

"Fanya Ivanowna!—You?"

"Sh-h-h !" Fanya tried to stop her. Too late.

"Fanya Ivanowna!" Mary Porter, an old friend she hadn't seen for years, shook her hand warmly. "What the devil are you up to now? Have you come to write us up?"

The employment manager gave Fanya one look, his brows drawn up high in astonishment. Then he turned to Miss Porter. "I'll see you later," he said in a tight voice.

Fanya followed him to his office. "What does this mean?" he demanded. "Do you know what a serious offense it is to try to get work under an assumed name?"

"Yes, I know."

He regarded her with hard-mouthed silence.

"The matter is dismissed."

Fanya rose, and then paused.

"Please—I just want you to understand. You see, at the last place I killed my chance by telling the truth—and so—"

His gaze remained fixed, far away. Fanya saw she was talking to a man no longer listening.

She turned and walked out.

Again rejected. In the eyes of business, she had been condemned again. She stood on the corner, in front of the store, staring bewildered—east, west, north, south. Where could she turn? What could she do next?

The tall buildings, the raucous rumble of traffic, the swirling mass of shoppers were part of the cruel force crushing her out. Like an animal in a trap she stood unable to see a way out.

CHAPTER XVI

Fanya sang to herself under her breath. She was dressed in a black uniform and a white apron, and this uniform, this garb of servitude, made her feel like a bird out of a cage. She had broken the spell of her incapacity, demonstrated the power to do what she wanted to do. She was actually working in a Sixth Avenue restaurant.

She picked up her tray. It was her turn to wait on the girls. She did it as naturally as that first day when she walked into the job as waitress.

"Hey! Fannie! Sneak us some chicken instead of that hash from yesterday," said Mill, the head waitress.

"And honey darling! Cream for the coffee!"

"Yeh! The cook's feeling fine. He'd give us squabs on toast for the asking."

Little screams of laughter rose from the table as the girls relaxed in their moment of freedom. While the boss was away, they went wild—like a crowd of youngsters in an orphan asylum escaped for a moment from the restraint of their matron.

"Gee! If the boss would only stay out! Our only chance for some decent grub. Let's make it a swell affair."

"Make it five on fruit cocktail!"

"Swipe us a couple of French pastries while you're about it!"

"Hold on! Wait a minute! One order at a time!" Fanya threw up her hands in happy excitement. "You kids'd send anybody crazy."

"Maybe we didn't get a kick in the teeth out of this," laughed Mill, crunching a chicken bone.

"Huh! I'm still hungry enough to eat gold fish," Agnes grumbled, pushing back her empty plate.

"I could chew a piece of linoleum and make believe it's sirloin steak," came from Mona, the blue-eyed, blond-haired vamp.

"Wolves!" Fanya scolded good-humoredly. "Your appetite will bankrupt the boss. I'm done with begging for this meal. How about you, Mona, giving cookie the glad eye?"

They all turned to Mona.

"Cleopatra, darling! Roll your eyes on your Mark Antony and work him for some ice cream."

"Say!" Mona flared. "Work him yourself."

"Aw, go on! You're the only one who *can.*"

"Sure, you know how to strut your stuff."

The door closed after her and they began:

"What do the men see in that calsomined lily, I'd like to know?"

"She's got plenty."

"It's the way she snakes her hips and looks the age of innocence."

"Sure!—they fall for a line like that."

"And how—is nobody's business."

Jealous whispers turned to squeals of delight as Mona approached with her full tray.

"Baby! You sure got It!"

"It takes a sky-piece like yours to wind Frank around your little finger."

While Mona was passing the dessert, Fanya, who faced the door, cried in a hoarse whisper, "Ssh-ssh! The boss!"

Faces paled. Laughter froze into silence. Mill gulped down a whole éclair. Agnes swept the chocolate cream into her pocket, ruining her fresh, white apron. By the time the boss came over, they were busy clearing tables, sorting linen, sweeping the floor— their "swell affair" submerged in an atmosphere of unbroken routine.

Frank was the only one who wasn't intimidated. The boss was always smiling to him, patting him on the back, treating him to brandy and wine, to keep him in good humor. There were other restaurants ready to snatch him up at any price. Knowing his value, Frank gave full sway to his temperament, and went as far as he liked with the girls.

Everyone knew about that red-haired waitress on whom Frank had a crush. She had pushed him away when he tried to kiss her. Swearing and cursing with gutter violence, he slammed the pots. At the height of the rush hour, when the girls began shouting their orders, he had flung a pan full of French fried potatoes on the floor.

The girls had scurried away like frightened mice. Frank raged like a prima donna. The brandy, the wine, the entreaties of the boss had no effect. Not until the girl was dismissed did he consent to fill out the orders again.

For days after, Frank was gentle as a lamb. He told the girls jokes, sang to them bits from the opera and shoved into their hands little extras of food.

But he couldn't cook unless he made love to some girl. And Mona was his favorite now.

He had given her the stolen favors with a full hand. But he hadn't done it for nothing. He was going to get his.

Half an hour later, as Mona dumped a tray of dishes into the sink, Frank, passing by, put his arm around her.

"You're a sweet little mama, baby."

Mona stiffened. He leaned closer and suddenly she felt his teeth on her neck.

"You dirty wop!" Mona slapped his cheek.

"You—you—high-hatting me!"

Little red threads darted out of his eyes as he seized her in his arms, kissed her lips.

With frightened strength, Mona twisted out of his arms and made for the pantry, where Fanya was arranging the salad.

"That bum!" she sobbed. "Wait, you'll see—he'll get me fired."

Fanya put her arms around her. Such a lovely, young thing. Those young blue eyes, made for joy and laughter, darkened with the worry for bread.

"You, with your looks—afraid of a job? You can get a dozen jobs."

"Jobs don't hang on bushes these days. I paid the Agency four dollars for this one. I'd have to pay again for another."

"Sure," added Agnes, trying to show her sympathy by telling her own hard luck. "Once they took my cash and sent me to a place that was already filled. But I don't let nobody do me dirt. I brought a policeman. You should have seen how quick they forked over the money."

The conversation came to a sudden halt. The boss came in to inspect the pantry and tell Mill of the new waitress that he had hired.

"That will give you girls a half a day a week off," he said with an air of conscious nobility.

As soon as he left, they all began to talk at once.

"My lands! What makes the little, white-haired boy so big-hearted all of a sudden?"

"A whole half-day off each week! How did he get that way?"

"It's that inspector," said Mill. "I heard him ask him about our day off.... Ha-ha! That's a good one! Our day off!... Anyway, it made him come across with a half-day."

"I don't know what the movies look like since I work here," said Mona, who was filling sugar bowls at a corner table. "The only kick out of life I can afford is window-shopping. Looking at clothes somebody else is going to buy."

"That reminds me—did I see a cute, little red hat at Hearns!" broke in Mill. "It sure was a tricky affair. That hat could knock anybody dead—and make them come to life again." Her mouth dropped open, her eyes half-closed with longing. "Gawd! If I could only wear that hat for my next date!"

Agnes always eating and always hungry, frowned impatiently. "You with your red hats—your glad rags! I'd be satisfied if we had decent meals. The only time I ever had enough was at the Civic Club. Think of it! The waitresses got the same grub as the club members. No tips. But oh boy! The presents we got on Christmas!"

"Catch me waiting all year for Christmas presents," scoffed Mill. "The real racket is in the speakeasies. That's where you pick up the jack. Just like velvet. I worked at a place once. A guy used to come there, a newspaper fella. As soon as he got happy, he'd peel off a dollar bill with every cocktail. Wasn't it a dirty shame for the cops to close up such a gold mine? By now, I could have had a fur coat or a diamond ring." She paused and looked about thoughtfully. "It sure is tough for a girl. This honest business don't pay."

With what innocent unconsciousness they poured themselves out, Fanya thought. No reserves. No knotty perplexities shut them off from one another. Unhampered by thought—unwasted by ambition. With all their troubles, they were so bright, so gay, so ready to turn into a "swell affair" the least chance for a good time. The hurts they suffered did not get under their skin to fester into discontent. Was it because they demanded less of life than she? And yet—how they loved life! The way the small things of the moment, something to eat, a date with a beau, the vision of a new hat so filled and diverted them that memory was obliterated.

They were like people born rich who are unaware that they're rich. Their ignorance was their wealth, their security. But was it ignorance—their freedom from the wasting fever of thought? This thinking and thinking—where did it get you? Into a sea without bottom, without shore. They made her feel how much easier and simpler life could be. They were born knowing what she had yet to learn—not to look back—not to strain forward—but to live *now—now*—and let God take care of tomorrow.

Every one of those first days was a new adventure. How startled she had been when she came in one morning and heard Frank sing "Pagliacci" in that rich resonant voice that swept the stove, the kitchen out of sight.

"You are Caruso come to life," she told him.

He smiled wistfully, almost saddened by her appreciation.

"I could've been Caruso. But a dame and her old woman roped me in. I got hitched up when I was eighteen. Before I knew it, I had a wife and kid to support. Now I've got three more. So I'll just stew in a kitchen for life."

He said it without complaint. Without any sense of tragedy. Just a fact. He had missed what he wanted most in life. Was it a wonder that he snatched at any momentary pleasure to forget? Were not his promiscuous love affairs casual clutching at forbidden joy, his way of seeking oblivion?

With her passion for sorrow and tragedy, she read sorrow and tragedy everywhere—even in the dumb smile of the dishwasher—a distant relative of the boss. A boy of nineteen. Because he was dumb and green and helpless, the boss paid him seven dollars a week. From six in the morning till eleven at night, he stood stooped over the sink—the sweat pouring from his face, his neck, his bare breast—his hands steeped in greasy suds, washing, washing endless stacks of dishes. Every time she passed him, his eyes cried to her. Those dumb, immigrant eyes. The look of a stranger in a strange land.

Sympathetically, she touched his shoulder and said: "Why don't you strike for an hour off? In America, everybody takes time to breathe."

He lifted faun-like, pleading eyes of a drudge who asks nothing, expects nothing but to be allowed to serve. "Oi-i-i! I love the sink! In the farm, from where I come, who had seen water running from a wall?" He pointed to the faucets. "A push of that—and there you got it—hot or cold. In the old country I had to pull up every pail of water from a well and then carry it a mile to the house."

She swung open the door of the kitchen—and there was life again in a different setting. Fanya learned to divine people's souls by what they ate—how they ate—the stray bits of conversation caught here and there.

Every day, at exactly twelve o'clock came the German widow, with her poverty-worn face, in her rusty, old black. She was said to be worth a million in real estate. But wealth had come too late to disturb her habits of frugality. To leave a scrap of bread, an olive, or a bit of pudding that she had paid for in her table d'hôte dinner was an unbearable waste. So, with conscious virtue, she stuffed down the very last morsel, regretfully leaving the ice in her glass.

"The bloody miser!" Mill hissed after her, as she saw the woman go without leaving a tip.

Another customer entered. A woman of indefinite years in a black and white checked suit, a few sizes too small. Over-rouged, over-perfumed. A black velvet tam framing a halo of bleached blond hair. A slightly soiled white fox scarf and a gilt mesh bag. She removed dirty white gloves, lit a cigarette, and ordered fruit cocktail, pastry, and coffee. Her hard, mirthless face gazed at emptiness through clouds of smoke.

Suddenly she straightened in her chair. A young girl came in, followed by a young man. He removed her wrap with a caressing, lingering touch at which the girl looked up and laughed a low, joyous laughter. Only one who has never known doubt or fear could laugh like that. A childlike trust that all was well with the world flowed like sunlight from her face. A face that needed no rouge. Ripe, fresh lips that needed no lipstick. Life, to her, was a gay party with always some charming man at her feet to make love to her.

The other woman's gaze fixed in an icy smile. Her mouth twisted in a grimace of contempt. She turned away sharply—and then back again, drawn by the irresistible freshness of youth. The hardness dropped from her eyes. Some memory seemed suddenly to have wrung her awake with pain.

Fanya, gently placing the bill on the table, roused the woman from her reverie.

She opened the gilt bag, drew out pawn tickets, a nickel, and a few pennies. "My Gawd!" She laughed uneasily. "I forgot to go to the bank."

With a bold stride, she walked over to the cashier's window and asked to be trusted.

"I might as well kiss it good-bye," said the boss, tearing up the check after she had left. "Her kind never pay. If she ever comes, send her to me."

A few days later the woman returned. In spite of the boss's orders, Fanya served her dinner. Then, to her amazement, the woman held out a five-dollar bill. "I owe you for last time," she reminded.

"That's one on me," the boss grinned, as he changed the money. "But I'd have given you hell, if she hadn't paid."

"If worse came to worst, I'd have paid it myself."

There was a swift raising of his eyelids as he looked at her.

"Well—well—but in the future don't trust your hunches."

Fanya smiled a non-committal smile. Why argue with the boss? He saw the restaurant in terms of checks, in the number of lunches and dinners sold. To her, it was a passing show of all kinds of people. And beneath this passing show? The unstilled, unceasing want—want—want in people's hearts, like a sea beating against rock barriers. Here behind the noisy irrelevance of their chatter, something invisible, intangible ever beckoned to her.

It was following her "hunches" about people, the occasional scent of the personal that made her life as a waitress so exciting. Faces, eyes, a smile—a turn of the lips, a tone of the voice had for her worlds of hidden meaning. The great moments came when some unconscious, self-revealing expression, some unseen, unspoken gesture in an individual, suddenly made her aware of the unseen, unspoken humanity under the raucous hum and clatter of eating and talking.

Once, at the dinner hour, a distracted young man stumbled in. His wild, unhappy eyes seemed unaware of anything around him.

"Coffee! Strong coffee, please," he ordered.

"Anything more?" Fanya asked.

"Nothing but coffee."

When she returned, his head was sunk in his hands. She put down his cup close beside him, but he did not see it.

"Are you ill?" she asked.

The anxiety in her voice made him look up.

"Ill? Huh!... I'm a man in hell." He stared at her with somber intensity. Despair looked out of his eyes. "Sure I'm in hell!... Serves me right."

The thickness of his voice, the complete lack of restraint made her wonder whether it was drink or despair talking in him. In his rambling way he told her his story. He was a poet. He had met the woman who became his life, the flame of all his poetry. They became so indispensable to each other that in spite of his free love theories they married. And then—his wife, a disciple of his own gospel of free love, went off with his best friend.

"They tell me I'll get used to it," he ended. "'Wait, you'll get used to it.'"

She leaned over, watching him in silence. Thoughts lost in dim shadows of her past stirred out of oblivion. Was she getting used to life without Henry Scott? Was she—so busy setting tables, carrying trays, taking orders—was she really drowning in noise, in confusion, in physical exhaustion—the silent sobbing of her heart?

She had stopped aching for him—even thinking of him—except to remember at every turn that she had ceased to think of him. Where was that veil of wonder, the something flaming and intense that lay over things when his face was the light before her eyes?

She had wanted to forget him. And now, the dull empty place in her heart—because she was forgetting him. Could love prove to be so shallow after all? Was this work making her so matter-of-fact that the fragile fragrance of love and longing was trampled down by routine?

His face was slipping from her, growing paler, dimmer, like the face of the dead, receding further and further away. Cutting bread, filling glasses with water, dishing out soup, every crowding task of the day was another clod of earth thrown over the beloved face fast sinking into the grave of forgotten things.

"Hey, kid! Are you playing hostess to a drunk?" Mill shook her by the sleeve. "They want you over there."

Fanya looked up. A fat, pouchy man motioned to her with his pudgy finger. "What you got in the line of desserts?"

She brought him the menu card. He glanced at it, then turned it over to his flabby wife.

"Well, dear? Which shall it be? Ice cream and cake? Or huckleberry pie?"

"Oh, well—" she pouted distractedly, her fingers glittering with diamonds, fumbled at the string of pearls beneath her double chins. "Pie'd be good. But—I was wanting some ice cream and cake. Oh, anything—suit yourself."

They ended by ordering huckleberry pie and ice cream. By the time Fanya returned from the kitchen, the unhappy poet had gone. A grey-haired woman sat in his place. A straight-backed schoolteacher. She ordered a lettuce sandwich and a cup of tea. Always the same lunch. She seemed insulated in an ether of silence. Always with the same don't-come-near-me smile that forbade approach. Always a book under her arm. While she ate, she read *The Conquest of Fear.*

Fanya served her gently, pitying her as one would an invalid, sick with shyness, with fear of people.

"Miss! Can you wait on me quick—please!" a young man's vibrant voice called. "I'm starved. Haven't eaten or slept in twenty-four hours."

Fanya turned, her swift glance taking in the buoyant brightness of the young face.

"What will you have?"

"Ham and eggs."

When she came back with his order, she found him smiling to himself like a man in love. Joy radiated from his eyes. The very air was alive with his life. He gulped down his food in huge mouthfuls, and talked as he ate.

"Rehearsing my play on Broadway. It's going great."

The fatigue of the long day vanished watching him, listening to him. This triumphant youth was like a bugle call from some far-off world to which she had once belonged. Though she was out of it—it still went on—the battle to achieve—the joy to bring forth and pass on what you saw and felt and lived.

"Fannie!" It was the boss's voice. "Bring me filet mignon, well-done."

Fanya's heart stopped talking to itself. She had to be there to wait on him. He loved to be waited on; he would choose a particular waitress, and watch her every move as she served him. Her job depended on her ability to dance attendance on him to his satisfaction; sometimes she would be chosen for a day, sometimes for as much as two weeks.

For the last week he had picked upon Fanya. A day or two ago he had taken to stroking her arm, where the short sleeve left it bare above the elbow, and telling her "You're a better looker than the rest." Fanya had managed not to shrink away—she was merely glad that he did it when none of the other girls were by. And while the greater part of her rebelled against this sort of thing, she could not help feeling that it put her into the swing of life again.

While he ate, the boss looked proudly round at the white tables, the shining silver, the flowers, the waitresses in their immaculate uniforms. He never said thank you. When he finished, he walked through the swinging doors into the kitchen to the cook.

"Old top! Your filet mignon is fit for John D." He

slapped Frank on the back. "That was some mushroom sauce. How do you do it?"

Frank grinned. "That's my secret. And I'm not telling."

The boss drew out his hip flask. "Have a swig?"

Frank helped himself.

"Have another," the boss urged magnanimously. "Another—only tell me how you make things touch the spot the way you do."

Warmed by the liquor, Frank's eyes brightened, the tenseness in his face relaxed. "You gotta know how—and you gotta be crazy about it. I get them coming because I got the stuff. King of the stomach—that's me."

He turned back to the stove—a monarch dismissing his subject. The boss smiled indulgently, watching him turn an omelette with breath-taking skill. Then he sauntered about with his pleased smile of ownership, watching the roast browning on the spit, one man carving chickens, another ladling soup. One girl by the refrigerator handing out salads—while the waitresses raced back and forth piling their trays.

He walked on to the lower kitchen where the red-faced, dripping pastry cook shoved pies into the oven. Two negro women, potato peelers, bent over huge pots. Their ragged waists exposed wrinkled black breasts. Always in the same position, making the same motion as they dropped the potatoes—one—another—another. The odor of negro sweat, steam of cooking filled the air.

The boss leaned down with the pastry cook to peer into the oven, glanced into the vegetable pots, strolled out leisurely, his benign smile exuding peace, content with himself and the world.

Endless was the pageant of life, the kaleidoscope of humanity between the kitchen and the dining room. Material enough for hundreds of stories—novels—plays. Here was the living stuff that cried for a new Dostoyevsky, a new Tolstoy to be born. Fanya saw it, felt it, but the power to express had vanished. Without Henry Scott she was dumb—impotent—a violin without a player—a hearth heaped high with fuel and no one to ignite it—a human being pulsing, sentient—bound to earth for want of one transforming breath of love.

If she could only see him. Then perhaps.... No. She must not think of him. Never. Never....

Resolutely she began to clear the tables and set them for the next meal. Presently the diners began to drop in. All thought was swept aside by the clamor for steaks and chops and dinners.

CHAPTER XVII

It was the early morning hour, when the humblest plodders hurried to their jobs—butchers, bakers, day laborers, factory hands. A group of street cleaners was clearing the dirt out of the gutter. Further on, grimy men with picks and shovels were excavating the ground for a new building. Fanya thought: when the outer differences that separate man from man are swept aside who shall say that the palettes of the painters and the chisels of the sculptors fill a deeper need of humanity than the brooms of these street cleaners and the picks and shovels of these ditch-diggers? These silent hordes in overalls, built with their hands the subways and skyscrapers. These hurrying human ants about her, lost to themselves, fed the world, clothed the world, housed the world. On their bowed backs was reared all the art of the world.

She saw one thread running through all things, uniting all people. Poetry, music, books, pictures—all the immortal stuff of life was rooted in the labor of these unknown mobs, swept with her to work.

While stooping to mop the floor of the restaurant, she felt in her self-abasement the glory of all the selfless toilers of the world. She thought of the folk tale of Uriel Akosta. Uriel was a youth whose ideas of God differed from those of the elders. So they excommunicated him. For a long time, he was able to live with himself in exalted isolation. He built himself a hut on a high hill, and communed all day with his high thoughts. Slowly, the need for human contact humbled him. His loneliness became so unendurable that he came, begging on his knees to be taken back into the fold. The stern elders imposed a penance for his pride. They commanded him to throw himself on the threshold of the temple and permit everyone who entered to step on him and spit on him. And so lonely, so hungry was he for the sight and sound of human beings that he was glad to fling to the winds all his dearly cherished ideas and ideals, glad to become a doormat under their feet, to be stepped upon and spat upon—only to feel again the wide, warm current of common people.

Her elation for work with others made her impervious, at first, to the close air, the stale food. The greasy hash of leftovers doled out to the waitresses would have revolted her if she had had to eat it alone. But the pleasure of the girls' company made her almost unaware of the slow poison she swallowed day after day. Excitement kept her going.

The girls revenged themselves on the boss by stealing from the portions served to customers. A stalk of celery, a mouthful of spinach, an asparagus tip, a bit of chicken, a slice of orange—anything and everything they could get hold of—they snatched to appease their hunger. Fanya knew their craving and despised herself for not having nerve enough to steal, too.

One day, just as Agnes was stuffing an asparagus tip into her mouth, the boss came upon her.

"What the hell is this?" he shouted. "Stealing from customers' plates?" He turned to the girls in the kitchen. "I want no thieves working for me. The next time I catch anyone—out you go."

Even after the boss's threat of dismissal, they kept on stealing, but more warily. They mocked Fanya for being too "ritzy" to help herself.

"Who do you think you are—Mrs. Gawd?" Mill scoffed when Fanya refused a piece of orange filched from a fruit cocktail.

Agnes came in, one morning, with a grey, sick face. She opened a bottle of citrate of magnesia and began swearing at the boss, as she drank down a glass of sizzling liquid. "The dirty skunk! Dumping all his garbage on us!"

She held out the bottle to the girls. "Who's next on this champagne?"

Fanya watched them drink the magnesia. Forced to take medicine when all they needed was food. Poisoned, starved, right in the midst of plenty!

Why had she drifted into this restaurant and become a waitress? It was to learn at first hand the terrible conditions under which the girls had to work. And then—fight to better their conditions. The long hours, the small pay, the degrading beggary of the tipping system was intolerable. No class of workers needed help so much as these defenseless, unorganized girls. She had come here to gather them together—rouse them out of their slavery—inspire them to demand their rights! Work had to be done much more important than writing books or cherishing a lost love. Everything she had been through had ripened her for this service. This, she told herself, was her reason for existence.

She saw herself going from restaurant to restaurant, recruiting the girls as in the great shirtwaist-makers strike, years ago. She saw the waitresses of the entire city, marching on Fifth Avenue—an army with banners.

At their usual lunch hour, Fanya sat down with the other girls at the back of the restaurant, to their usual meal: sour macaroni with bits of pork, greasy potatoes, fried for the third time.

"I can't touch this stuff!" Fanya burst out. "Here we've been serving chicken and chops and broth and fruit salad. Why should we have to eat this?"

The girls looked at one another and laughed.

"Sure, dearie!" snickered Mill. "Bring on the squabs in mushrooms."

"If we had the guts to demand decent food, we'd get it. Why should we be forced to steal from our customers, or wheedle Frank for a bite? One flower less on the tables would buy each of us a vegetable. Our food is part of our pay. We have a right—"

"Right, my eye," said Mona. "You think I want to lose my job? Go find another place—and you get it worse."

"Oh, you're just a bunch of slow ones," Fanya pushed back her plate. "How can you ever better your conditions unless you fight for them? It's not only us fighting for food—it's the workers all over the world."

"All right, kid! Tell it to the judge!"

"Tell it to the boss and get fired!"

"If you'd only get together!" The ardor of an impassioned labor leader at a mass meeting was in her voice. "Look at the Amalgamated Tailors! They went after it—and got it. Why can't we do the same?"

"Maybe this idea of getting together ain't so nutty," Agnes said. "It's hell to be hungry all the time."

Inflamed by the least sign of response, Fanya went on.

"Worse even than the rotten food and the long hours—is the degrading shame of the tipping system. We don't want tips!"

"No tips!" Jane hissed. "I like that! Where do we get off?"

Their tolerant amusement now grew into hostile resentment. Angry eyes turned on her.

"Wouldn't she jar your grandmother's preserves?" Mill buzzed behind her hand. "I've got a good mind to give the boss the dope on her."

"Only here a couple of weeks—and wants to lead the show."

"Too damn much nerve—that's what's the matter with her."

Mill's jealousy that had been gathering up in her from the day Fanya won the notice of the boss had found an outlet at last.

"No wonder our little white-haired boy leaves her in charge of the cash register instead of me. That oil-can had the brass to tell him she had three years experience. Yes," she scoffed, "three years' experience serving hot bologna in a steam laundry."

"If you would only stand by me—the whole bunch of you," Fanya exhorted, her cheeks flushed, her eyes aglow with the cause. "Life is for those who demand life." The resonance of her voice was like a fire that fed her. She looked far out—seeing prophecies. "Alone we're nothing. Together we're a power that can force the boss to do our bidding. Who's the boss, anyway? An ignorant bully—a fathead so dulled from overeating he can't see we're starving right before his eyes. The minute we'd show him we want what we want—we'd get it."

The murmur among the girls grew so shrill the kitchen help peeked through the door. In the meantime, Mill had slipped out unnoticed.

"How many of you are with me?" Fanya shouted, forgetting all caution in her enthusiasm.

"Rattlesnake!" shrieked the boss, bursting in. "I'll show you who's with you!"

Fanya's face turned pale, then red. Her gaze flashed from the boss to Mill who seemed not to see her. The girls sat motionless—eyes on the floor.

"Get the hell out of here! You hear me?" he vociferated, with menacing outthrust of his lower jaw. "Anyone else looking for rights?"

Fanya gave one last glance at the hushed, panic-stricken girls. They seemed so small, so defenseless against the bullying boss. She could hear their frightened breathing, feel the shivers of their cringing, cowering helplessness. Slowly, she put on her hat and coat. She heard the dishwasher piling the dishes. She heard the cook stirring the sauce. In the front, the door opened. A customer entered. This place—these people—they had become part of her. What did anything matter against the rich camaraderie she had enjoyed in that kitchen? She longed to cry out: I can't go. I can't! I belong here! But she only tightened her lips, lifted her head high and very slowly walked out.

CHAPTER XVIII

After her abrupt dismissal from the restaurant, Fanya walked the streets wondering what to do next. Inevitably her mind turned to him. Those busy months when she thought she was forgetting him, making a new life for herself, she had only been running away from the old life. Pushing the need of him from her. And now, it rushed back—a wild tide bursting through all resistance of reason.

She wandered on, dead to all that surged clamorously about her—jammed crossings, taxi horns, swirling crowds. The streets that had once been to her inspiration, life, were now a meaningless roar—a parade of shadows.

Suddenly, in the thick of the traffic, she saw him on the opposite side, coming toward her. His eyes were upon her, smiling. Impulsively her hands rushed out to the sunlight of his smile.

Then a whistle. A change of lights. A policeman clutched her from under the fender of a huge truck. When the jam subsided and she was allowed to pass on, he had vanished.

She walked home still seeing him. His smile before her all the way. Back in her lonely room, she sank in a chair, covered her eyes with her hand, but she could not shut him out. His eyes, his face encircled her.

Mechanically, her hand pulled open a drawer of her desk. There was the chaos of her countless attempts to write to him. Letters upon letters she had started and never finished.

She picked up a page. Coldly, dispassionately, she read the feverish effort of a sleepless night.

"In a far-off northern country, where for centuries the people were imprisoned in a barren waste of snow and ice, where nothing had ever happened to disturb the unending monotony of their ice-bound lives, there suddenly occurred a wondrous phenomenon of nature. The desert of snow and ice was swept away by an amazing interlude of spring.

"The sun began to shine, warming the frozen earth into a new birth. Green hillsides burst into bloom. Islands of bluebells, violets, and arbutus sprang up in the creeks that broke free from ice-locked streams. Brooks and waterfalls tumbled and laughed through blossoming fields. Gay-colored birds built their nests in the trees. The infinite variety of nature opened a thousand eyes, spoke in a myriad voices of joy in life.

"And just as the people gazed in breathless wonder at the revelation of a new-born world—lo! It was gone. With unwilling, unbelieving eyes they beheld again the white silence closing in on them, slowly stifling their lives.

"Although the snow and ice had been all they had ever known from the beginning of time, and the interlude of spring but as a day, yet that one, warm, golden day remained the only living part of their existence.

And the cold, barren years behind and before them
but a prison that held that one day... "

The page crumpled in her hand. The way she had
burned creating the story. And here it moldered in the
drawer with a hundred other futile scrawls.

Her eyes closed. Through tired lids she watched the
dim drama of a dream.

Again she looked into the cool, sane face. He sat in
his kingdom of books. His office, lined from the floor
to the ceiling with volumes of psychology, philosophy, and sociology. What a chance had her wavering,
chaotic soul against these rows of massive wisdom?
Her confused emotion—against his clear, disciplined
intellect?

"I can't give them up," she pleaded, clutching the letters he wanted back. "If I can't have you, let me at least
hold onto your words. The only light in my darkness."

"My dear, don't spend yourself uselessly. You lavish
yourself upon me and I don't deserve it. These letters
must be destroyed."

"It's cruel to destroy them. Look at this. The way you
addressed me: 'Dear love of God'! If you deny me, you
deny God."

"Oh, don't. Don't. We can't afford to be tragic—"

"What do you expect of me? You no longer trust me.
These letters—don't rob me of them!"

"Unthinkable. Understand, this is a very delicate
matter to me. Suppose this were found out?"

"What if it were found out? Why hide it?"

"You must grow up. Look at all this sanely. Learn to
be reasonable."

Sane! Reasonable! Crawling, earthbound worms!

Fanya tore herself violently out of her waking trance. She had imagined all that happening because the actual facts were so unbearably sordid. She had to create this scene for herself to escape the horrible anti-climax of their love.

She had not given up the letters—even though he had asked for them. She had clung to them. Clung to them against reason. Against her deepest sense of loyalty. There they were, still in her trunk.

Even after he had gone off on an educational mission to Mexico, she did not for a moment think it was the end. And while he was away she had written a book to him, for him.

As soon as it was published, she sent it to him. "See! I've done the impossible for you. Here's the cry of all the lost people back of me. I've plucked out the chaos of my soul for you."

No answer. Still she couldn't believe it was the end.

There was in her a power that he had dug up out of the confusion that wasted her. He himself had put that power in her hands. How could he help being interested in the way she used the gift he had discovered?

He had returned when the screen production of one of her novels was completed. Now she had an excuse to see him. To invite him to the first showing of her picture.

"I have so much to do," he explained, refusing the invitation. "I won't be able to leave my lecture."

After an awkward pause, he said, quietly, "My letters. Will you return them to me?"

She looked at him in terror. "They're mine. Mine."

Blindly she groped for the door.

In the street, a confused sense of guilt and shame stopped her. "They're not mine, if he wants them back.... Mine—his? But his letters are mine," she cried in defiance of all reason. "He never wrote poetry before. I made a poet of him. His letters could not have come into existence without me. They're mine. What are all his books on sociology? Abstractions. In his letters he'd live forever. A great man capable of great love."

She rose from her desk. Gathered up the loose pages that filled the drawer. All the thousand gestures toward him of which he would never know. She put them in the fireplace, lit a match and held it against the papers till a flame rose above them.

She watched without emotion the flame eating into black ashes the futile, incommunicable expression of her love. She could destroy her letters to him. Because they came from a selfish need.

But his letters! They belonged to those rare documents of humanity that shed upon the dark confusion of this world a new light. They spoke of a new day to come "when every valley shall be exalted, the blind shall see, the dumb shall speak. And the first and last be one with God."

When she finally fell asleep, she dreamed they were together on the college campus in front of the gilt statue of Alma Mater. He was showing her the owl of wisdom hidden in the folds of Alma Mater's gown.

Students in black mortarboard caps and long black gowns were walking up and down the broad library steps. Chirping sparrows were flying low in the sun. Some were taking dust baths in the warm gravel. Some were drinking out of the big, stone fountain. Clear water shot up from the basin and fell fanwise, catching the light so that rainbows played in the streaming drops.

"Come," Fanya whispered, pulling him away from the statue. "Leave wisdom behind you. Let's drink this rainbow and fly away like birds of the air."

He did not answer. He only drew her closer to him, enfolding her in his gaze. All at once one of his colleagues passed, beckoned to the others. They stood in a row, pointing and shaming them with their fingers.

"Oh, they're seeing us!" he cried, in alarm. "Seeing us with their eyes. Discussing us with their cynicism."

Even as he talked, he withdrew from her, his glance colder and colder. He thrust her from him into a black void but still she held onto him.

Suddenly his repulse pierced her through and through. She was too spent to struggle back to him. All she wanted was to be free. Free from the man who did not want her.

She let go her hold of him and fell swiftly down—down.

She woke from the torment of her dream with a strange clarity of mind that seemed the culmination of all her waking thought.

In the morning, she made a bundle of his letters, called a special messenger to deliver them. The last moment, she wrote a note:

"My Friend,

I should have returned these letters years ago when you asked for them, but I was like a person with only one light in the room, afraid of the dark."

This note she placed on top of the package.

He did not answer. About a week later, she went to the telegraph office to make sure that the letters had reached him. They showed her his signature.

CHAPTER XIX

The return of his letters failed to bring the peace for which Fanya had hoped. She would wake up in the middle of the night—and there was weeping in her heart.

Again, as in all her dark hours, Fanya sought Helena Hoffman.

The library was crowded as usual. Fanya looked about.

"Where's Miss Hoffman?" she asked the librarian at the desk.

"She's home for the day."

"If she stayed at home on a weekday, she must be ill," Fanya thought, hurrying off to see her.

On the way she passed a florist shop with a pail of pink cosmos in the doorway. Fanya stopped to buy a bunch.

With the paper-wrapped bouquet under her arm, she rang the bell.

"Well—well—what good wind brought you here?" Miss Hoffman led Fanya to an inviting armchair near the window.

A bowl of marigolds on an old mahogany table. An open bookshelf, with the books offering themselves. Orange and brown pillows tumbled on a low couch.

Low comfortable chairs. Each piece in that room seemed so simple and matter-of-fact and yet together—what a restful picture.

"I thought you were ill." And, tearing off the paper, she presented the flowers.

"Don't you know it's the Day of Atonement?"

"Day of Atonement?" Fanya stared at Miss Hoffman in astonishment. "You mean to tell me you still keep up the old holidays?"

"Of course I keep them. These holidays are so bound up with my early bringing up—my father's reverence for Jewish traditions."

"Your father ... "

As Miss Hoffman talked, memories crowded in upon Fanya. The synagogue: in her native village in Poland, on the Day of Atonement. Her father and other Jews of the village dressed in white shrouds and white stockings—praying, ceaselessly praying. Beginning at sundown, and for twenty-four hours, without food, without sleep, beating their breasts, abasing themselves as they swayed, chanting prayers before the throne of Jehovah.

The solemnity, the awe of those suppliant figures, raising their voices in one voice, year after year, generation after generation, century after century.

The Day of Atonement brought up the vision of her father. That frail, old, white-haired man! What strength radiated from him even in his hours of weakness. Even when racked by illness the look of his saintly face as he sat up in bed, propped by pillows, books all around him, chanting the beloved psalms of his beloved *Torah*:

Lift thine eyes unto the hills
Whence cometh thine aid—

And even when disease seemed to overcome him.
His eyes failed. His voice failed. He could no longer sit
up and chant, his heroic face, as he lay on the straw
mattress of their humble little home, accepting the end.

Even then, the people of the village and the villages
all about who flocked to his bedside did not come to
console, to pity, but to be inspired, to be unbound
from their everydayness. Merely looking into his great,
quiet eyes filled them with something beyond this
world, beyond this life.

That Sabbath morning when her father was dying.
The doctor felt his pulse, gave one meaningful look,
the end had come.

Suddenly, her father's frail, weak body stirred out
of coma. His eyes opened wide, turned to her mother—
eyes of a man whose spirit had always triumphed over
his body. He made a sign for her to come closer.

"Shabbes!" he murmured. "Shabbes!"

Her mother nodded back to him. The neighbors watching nodded to one another in silence. They knew what
he had meant to say. He would not die on the Sabbath.
There must be no burial among Jews on the Sabbath.
For even God and His angels must keep holy the day of
rest. With the indomitable spirit of his race he kept the
breath in his frail, dying body till after sundown.

Suddenly, Fanya became aware of her father's undy-
ing spirit in her. The going on in her of his race, which
was her race.

"How could I have forgotten the Day of Atonement?"

Fanya turned to Miss Hoffman. "All these years I have gone about a little bit ashamed of my manners, my background. I was so eager to acquire from the Gentiles their low voices, their calm, their poise, that I lost what I had—what I was."

She paused, trying to grasp her own thoughts. "I was clutching so greedily at the rainbow that I lost the reality. Why, the mere thought of my father is ground under my feet, a sky over my head."

Helena Hoffman put her hand gently on Fanya's. "Now that you have found yourself in your father you have found something real and abiding. Roots to hold you. Soil in which to grow."

Fanya walked over to the window. Before her spread the city, roofs, towers, bridges, skyscrapers. The city from a height. How infinite, how many-sided was the beauty of the world! She had thought that beauty, strength, power was only in and about Henry Scott. Now she knew that beauty was everywhere. Some of it very old like the imperishable beauty of her father. And some, like the tranquil isolation of this woman— taking into her heart her people.

Fanya turned back to Miss Hoffman. "I've been Israel in the wilderness making a false image."

"But now, the Day of Atonement has brought you back among your own."

"Yes. But there's one thing I feel I must do. I must go to him and talk it all out with him, before I can be free to go on."

Miss Hoffman gave a low, little laugh. "Who was it said that the curse of the human race is hope?"

"I do not hope for anything. I only want to say good-bye to love before I bury it forever."

"*Noch am grabe pflantzt er die Hoffenung!*" She smiled sadly at Fanya.

"Yes. Even on the grave man plants his hope," Fanya returned. "I still believe that he and I can at least part as friends. I'm ten years older now."

Miss Hoflman pointed to a Rodin figure on her desk. "You might as well expect that statue to walk over to you as to expect anything more of Henry Scott. He has given you all he had to give. And now—"

But Fanya had ceased to listen. She smiled softly to herself. Her eyes far away. And slowly across her ravaged face came that illumination so bright, so transforming that all the terrible fingering of the years changed into a pattern of loveliness.

Helena Hoffman rose from her chair, touched the flowers Fanya had brought her. This light upon Fanya's face terrified her. She looked at the younger woman for a moment, her eyes veiled, her gaze impassive. Then, with sudden compassion, she took Fanya into her arms.

"Forgive me. Who am I to know what is best for you?"

That day, Fanya wrote to him, asking for an appointment.

CHAPTER XX

The hands of the clock moved slowly. Ten minutes before two. Time enough to make her escape. Escape? Where was the revelation of the Day of Atonement? Rows upon rows of books—thick, brown, and dusty—seemed to wall her in. She would go. No, she would stay. But why stay? Miss Hoffman was right. Hope was more devastating than fear.

Gradually, she became aware of the room, the people about her. This was the special reference library, used by those who were preparing theses in sociology. Beyond, in the corner, was the locked door leading to his private office.

Grave-eyed young men and women peered into formidable volumes. Some were taking notes, crouched behind piles of bulletins and encyclopedias. They plodded from page to page with joyless faces. Now and then one of them paused, glanced about the room with a look of great importance. The hard breathing of laborious study filled the air.

Once more her eyes turned to the clock. A new fear swept away every other emotion. She half rose—only to fall back helpless with indecision. This agony of waiting— She had drawn on her last strength to prepare for the meeting, but this—this waiting...

A sound of footsteps! The blood rose to her cheeks and burned its way slowly to her temples. She tore herself out of her fear to look up. Oh, oh-h-h! Only a student. The panic receded, but her nerves were still tight with suspense.

She opened her purse to look into the little mirror that had remained unused ever since she had bought the bag. Perhaps she should have dressed for the occasion. There were people with enough detachment to dress when they go to a funeral to bury their dead.

The amazing thing, as soon as she got his note, was that she had rushed to her dressing table to see how she looked. Gone the brightness of her hair, the smooth freshness of her skin. A beauty parlor? Proper make-up might still hide or soften the harsh greyness of the years. She smiled wryly at herself. He was sixty-five, years older than she. And yet she considered him young compared to her. He had the poise, the will to breast the current of life, while she was driftwood in the tide, battered on the rocks.

Two o'clock! She stirred restlessly in her chair. Curious eyes were turned on her. She saw nothing but the clock. Her eyes were fastened on the minute hand. Five minutes past two. Ten minutes past. He wasn't coming.

Twenty minutes late! And still she waited. Turning from the clock to the door—and from the door back to the clock.

Ten years ago, when the research group was being disbanded and they were packing their things to go home, she had stolen into his room while he was out

for lunch. To touch his things for the last time. To
take leave of the room, the air he breathed. Her hand
ran through the things packed in his open valise. His
Japanese black and gold robe was on a chair. With swift
fingers, she snatched it and held it against her cheek.

"Good-bye! Good-bye!" She sobbed into the folds
the grief she dared not show him. Then without knowing how—why—she ran with it into her room and hid
it in her trunk.

Something to hold that was his, still alive with his
breath. How impatiently she had waited till she got
to her room in New York. Without stopping to unpack,
her hand felt for the stolen treasure at the bottom of
the trunk. In a moment she had it on—only to tear it
from her—burned alive. Fire was in the thing he had
worn. She could never wear it, nor return it to him.
She could not bear it in her room.

Late that night, in an empty lot, she burned it. And
as she watched the sparks fly, it seemed that her heart
and her body went up into the flames. . . .

"I'm sorry I'm late." The voice came to her across a
vast abyss. He had come. She felt herself rise without
legs. And now—to plunge through the faintness, the
fear—and dare face him.

As he turned to unlock the door, she tried to steal
a side glance at his face. But all these years, nursing
in her imagination his unreal, dreamlike existence,
forced her eyes to escape helpless. She could see nothing but unreality. The whole object of her quest—he—
she—the very thought of any comradeship between
them turned into a phantom—an obliterated memory.

With no further word than his incommunicable, cool smile, he held open the door for her.

He followed her in, pointed to a chair near his bookcase. Still politely aloof, he drew his own chair away from the desk, seated himself, and turned coolly toward her.

"I didn't want to come," she blurted out. "But when I did come—" She paused, her lips dry, unable to force another word out of her tight throat.

He smiled his cool smile. Serene, aloof, he kept his distance beautifully. She saw him take her in with the eyes of the psychologist—eyes of appraisal.

His eyes wandered to the stack of mail on his desk. Unconsciously, he began to slit open the envelopes. She was merely a stranger now—intruding upon the routine of his work—a stranger who might step upon the threshold, but not enter—one who might even be listened to courteously—but to be dismissed as soon as possible.

Fanya felt as if she were watching something not actually happening. A play on the screen—on the stage. Or was she merely visualizing one of the scenes that her fancy was forever weaving around him?

What was the word for his face? Full-blown. Rooted. Yes, he was as rooted in life, in the world about him as a full-grown tree was rooted in the earth. It had gone well with him—and he showed it. Success had heightened his magnetism.

The telephone rang. He took up the receiver eagerly—too eagerly.

"Oh yes, Miss Foster. I can see you shortly. When do you want to come?"

While the conversation went on, her swift eye caught sight of one of her books on the crowded shelf. Her first book. She picked it up, opened it. The pages weren't even cut.

She sat back very still, watching him from under lowered lids, as he talked into the mouthpiece.

For an instant she saw him with clear eyes. A stranger. As casual as someone glanced at and passed by in the street. And she had set him up in her heart as the image of love and understanding. She had as much reason to expect a response from the sphinx in far-off Egypt.

All at once it came to her, "Have I ever understood him?"

Everybody wanted to be understood. He wanted it no less than the illiterate Italian at the fruit stand on the corner. How could she ever know the myriad ways in which she had failed him?

It was as though she had come here in her sleep and suddenly opened her eyes, and seen in a revealing flash the gulf between them—how immeasurably far apart they were—had always been.

The outrageous egotism of wanting to use this man's life for her wishes, no matter how fine and noble her wishes were! For the assuagement and exaltation of her little ego she had wanted him to flow into the image of her blind desire—change the pattern of conduct that five generations of New England farmers had built up in him. He could no more step out of his New England mold than she could escape the forces that made the timbre of her voice or the color of her eyes.

Yes. That was his chief advantage over her. He knew himself. He knew he was a Yankee puritan. And therein lay his strength. She sought escape from what she was. Therein lay her weakness. Deserting the people back of her. Abandoning the God of her fathers. Setting him up as her new god. Dreaming of a love that never was!

She saw him glance at his watch as he talked into the telephone.

"Well, I can have time for you in about fifteen or twenty minutes."

He hung up and turned back to her. Fifteen minutes!

And how she had rehearsed what she would say. Fifteen minutes! Time was almost up. And her thoughts and the words for her thoughts were as far apart as he and she.

Through the panic of silence that locked her lips, her thoughts revolved like a spinning-top.... Who knows, perhaps his I-am-out-of-it smile was a mask hiding a deeper tumult than her own? The mask of the Anglo-Saxon who meets disappointment, frustration as though it were of no more concern to him than a little more or less sugar in his coffee.

"I sort of wonder—" she stumbled, awkwardly. "Have you read my last book?"

"No, you see I'm very busy," pointing to his crowded desk, with knitted brows, as though worried with work waiting to be done.

"And the book before? The publishers—they wrote you—wanted your opinion—"

"I get so many books from publishers. If I stopped to read them all, when would I get my own work done?"

Her book one of the "many books sent by publishers"! Still she went on talking, unable to endure the silence and too bewildered to know how to end the interview.

"One reason I came, I have been considering applying for the Mona Vale scholarship. Nothing is required except proof of creative ability. And I thought a new environment—"

"Yes. That's a good idea." His calm voice had no mercy on her.

"Perhaps because I've never been to college, I feel so unsure of myself." She paused, suddenly switched from the trend of her words. "Where am I?" She smiled feebly, staring into space." Oh, I shouldn't have come to bother you—but—I thought you might know something about the Mona Vale scholarship—"

"Yes. By all means. It would be worth your while to get it."

"Thank you," she said, gathering up purse and gloves. Her eyes measured the distance to the door. To escape alive from the horror, the unreality of two ghosts making dead conversation.

"Good afternoon," came the dead monotone, holding open for her the door. "I wish you all the success in the world."

CHAPTER XXI

Exhausted, like a spent runner, she walked slowly down the steps. A dreamer awaking from her dreams.

Not only had he no need of her, she knew now that she had no more need of him. She was free at last from the futile obsession of her dependence on him. Alone. Face to face with "that last strange peace whose name is loneliness."

A secret was at hand. She was about to lay her finger on something she had sought to understand all her life. The clue to that inescapable isolation from which she had tried in vain to escape.

No two people ever really touched each other. Mother and child—the nearest and dearest born of one flesh, never quite merged. There must be a reason for the impassable profundities between race and race. Something unripe, unfinished in Gentile and Jew keeps them from fulfillment—except in art—except in dreams.

Out on the campus, she met Miss Foster.

"Miss Ivanowna! Where have you been all these years? Oh, but why so sad?"

Fanya straightened up. There was Miss Foster as immaculately groomed as ever, in her blue tailored suit and close-fitting turban. Ten years had only enhanced the poise and power of her sure personality.

"Coming to the affair tonight?"

"What affair?" Fanya asked.

"Don't you read the daily papers?"

"There are so many things one ought to do and doesn't."

Miss Foster opened the front page of the *World* and handed it to Fanya.

The old excitement returned as his picture leaped at her. She read the headlines:

"Henry Scott Honored. Dinner by pupils and friends at the Plaza Hotel. Unveiling and presentation of portrait at Booth Theatre."

"I wrote you when we were sending requests for contributions," said Miss Foster. "Probably to the wrong address. For the letter came back."

"May I make my contribution now?" Swiftly Fanya opened her handbag and took out all the bills she had, just as he had emptied his purse for her, long ago. Life could still be kind to give her this sudden chance to reciprocate.

Miss Foster stood gaping in amazement at the sudden light in Fanya's eyes, as she hurried away.

At the first news stand, Fanya stopped and picked out a morning and an evening paper, with the story about him. Then opening her bag, she remembered she hadn't a cent.

"Won't you please trust me with this and some carfare?"

The man looked at her. Unprotesting, he gave her

the papers and her carfare, staring after her with something of the same expression that had been in Miss Foster's face.

In her room, she spread the papers out on the bed and read all about his new triumph.

Not until she was in the lobby of the Plaza and saw the people crowding into the elevator marked "Henry Scott Dinner," did she realize how formal the affair was to be. Businessmen, educators, artists, scientists, the prominent men and women of the country had come to honor him.

In her imagination, her thoughts resounded through the ballroom—stirring every heart of the crowd.... "Which of you know what it is to be crippled with a beggar's bag on your neck—and then meet someone great enough, loving enough, to see you whole—someone who says to you: 'You suffer as if you are dumb and stifled. You suffer from striving. You desire to be. You are: but you do not yet fully know that you are. And perhaps I can have the happiness of helping you realize that you are and what you are.'

"Oh, if you knew what it means to one sinking in the darkness of poverty, to be suddenly taken to the heights and see all of life stretching before you a great, beautiful infinity of love."

At the threshold of the reception room, she paused. He stood at the head of a long line waiting to shake his hand. Never before had she seen him in evening clothes. The black broadcloth set off the snow-white hair, the lofty head of the thinker. Never had she seen his face so luminous. And again she thought, how can

the beauty of youth compare to the mellowed radiance
of his face?

Suddenly, she felt his eyes on her. His look of appre-
hension—cold and sharp as steel—shot through her,
nailing her against the wall. Was it fear—was it hate
she saw in that look?

It was too late to make her escape now. To walk out at
this moment was to expose herself again to his notice.
So she let herself be carried off by the crowd to one
of the side-tables. Her eyes burned through the guests
about the speakers' table, vainly seeking his eyes.

He made no sign. Not a gleam of recognition. He had
ceased to see her.

All at once Fanya saw an exit behind the waiters'
screen and swiftly made her escape.

In the street, doubt of herself assailed her. Perhaps
it wasn't fear and hate she saw in his eyes, but shame
and embarrassment. He who had it in him to be a St.
Francis of Assisi, brother of the poor, the oppressed—
giving it up to be the idol of society...

But was he giving it up? He was big enough to be
friend of the rich no less than the poor. The whole
world revolved around him. Women's loves, public
acclaim, the limelight of the press beat against him
like surf against granite. Neither the adulation of
this mob nor the censure of his critics touched him—
because he was as focused on his work as a star in its
course.

A resistless urge overrode her exhaustion and
drove her to the theatre where the portrait was to be
unveiled. The only seats left were in the gallery.

She was just in time to hear the chairman end the introduction with, "I shall call upon Professor Rogers, his colleague and lifelong friend, who in words specially fitting the occasion will speak to us of our beloved leader."

Storms of applause broke about her. Every neck in that gallery craned for a sight of Henry Scott.

Adjusting her opera glasses to her eyes, she saw him in front of the stage, radiant, graciously accepting the ovation.

Professor Rogers began, but she barely saw or heard him, so absorbedly did she watch every passing shade of expression on Henry's face.

"We liberals are facing a crisis of uncertainty and confusion. We seem to be drifting. We know not where. In a time when all our ideals seem changing and dissolving—Henry Scott stands like a spiritual landmark, a steadfast light pointing the way. A pioneer and a radical, so profound that scholars throughout the country eagerly await his pronouncements. Foremost as a thinker when a young man—and now at three score and five still leading our youth. He keeps his head clear above the turmoil of the moment. He can't be confused. He has been big enough to work with the social forces of his time without yielding himself up to them."

Fanya raised the opera glasses. His face in the tiny circle was quite close to her—that strange familiar face—now passing forever out of her life to wider horizons.

He had his world. She had hers.

"A saint in his personal life—an Anglo-Saxon to the core in his championship of the underdog," the speaker's voice went on. "He has given himself generously to every cause of the people as opposed to the power of the ruling class—to free speech—the rights of labor—to racial equality. And he has fought—not as a rebel—a partisan, but as a statesman—a prophet, with authority and prestige.

"In gratitude for his vision and leadership, his students and friends are presenting to him, and indirectly to the art world, his portrait done by Kahlil Gibran, an artist of international fame." And he unveiled the painting.

The whole house shook with tumultuous applause, "Henry Scott! Henry Scott!" Like one peal of thunder crashing into another was the clapping and cheering. With gracious acceptance of their adulation, he rose, smiled at the audience. Everyone strained to see the rugged, earnest face, the shining eyes with their look of furtive trust.

"The veil ought to be over me instead of over the portrait," he said in his quiet voice. "I feel like one who has listened to his own funeral oration, in which all the conventional virtues were attributed to me and all the little foibles and follies that made me human to the few intimates who knew me, were discreetly ignored.

"Success like failure is but a mask thrust upon us perforce. Look beneath the passing show and you see that the exalted hero of the hour, or the condemned criminal, is but the accident of circumstances. The real man—who knows the real man except those who can see him stripped of his failures and successes?"

He paused and his hands went into his pockets in their accustomed way.

"While I was sitting for my portrait, I became very much interested in the artist's method of work. His rare combination of mental fixity and physical mobility. I could not see myself, but I felt that he had seized hold of the real me—that the portrait looked as I felt. One morning, when the picture was nearly finished, I asked him:

"'Well, how is it going?'

"'There isn't a moment that I don't curse myself because I don't know more,' was his reply. 'I have never yet gotten a face the way I wanted it.'

"'Yes, I know,' I said. 'In all my life I have never done the thing I wanted in the way I wanted it done.'"

The smiles of the audience encircled him.

"Will you consider that I have said everything that I should have said," he ended. "I thank you all once more."

In the street, the whole evening dissolved like the gossamer stuff of a dream. A tide of unreality seemed to sweep over every cherished memory. She stood with dim eyes, seeing him borne away in a sea of oblivion, among the fading faces of the beloved dead.

Out of that white mist of nothingness leaped in letters of fire lines of his first poem to her—

> Generations of stifled worlds, reaching out
> > *through you,*
> > Aching for utterance, dying on lips
> That have died of hunger,
> > Hunger not to have, but to be.

Generations as yet unuttered, dumb, inchoate,
   Unutterable by me and mine,
In you I see them coming to be,
   Luminous, slow-revolving, ordered in rhythm.
You shall not utter them; *you shall be them.*
   And from out thy pain
A song shall fill the world.

The words seemed to open and spread their meaning all about her like sunrise, spreading upon earth the light of a new day.

Her feet led her back to the ghetto streets where they had walked together when she first knew him. It was summer then. The air alive with the hum of people, standing in the doorways, sitting on the stoops, sprawled about on the sidewalks, leaning out of the windows. Seward Park was packed with the crowd waiting to hear music.

Now, an icy wind had driven the people from the streets. The park stood bleak and still, deserted by all who had once warmed themselves in its sun and cooled themselves in its shade. The fountain where once the children had splashed so joyously was now lifeless stone, shrouded in snow. Trees stood gnarled and stiff like skeletons, weighted down with sleet and ice. Even the tenements, surrounding the park, stared at her lonely and forlorn.

She walked on, searching the streets, for what she knew not. All at once she paused. The quavering strain of an old, familiar chant came from somewhere nearby.

"O Lord my God, I cried unto Thee and Thou hast O Lord, Thou hast healed me."

Through a grimy, basement window Fanya saw an old rabbi with a long, white beard. A Chanukah candlestick with one lighted candle threw uncanny shadows about his rapt face, as he sat leaning over the Bible, swaying and chanting in Hebrew:

"O Lord. Thou hast brought up my soul from the grave; Thou hast kept me alive that I should not go down into the pit."

In his uplifted eyes Fanya saw her father. And the long line of men who made her father. The psalm he chanted was the psalm her father had chanted years ago in celebration of the Festival of Lights.

"Weeping may endure for a night, but joy cometh in the morning," . . . the song went on.

The little village in Poland where she was born suddenly flashed into life. Her father, holding forth, surrounded by neighbors. How their narrow kitchen walls stretched out into far-off lands when he related the miracles and wonders of long ago.

"The Festival of Lights shines down the ages in remembrance of our liberty from Antiochus Epiphanes who had set up a graven image in the altar of the temple in Jerusalem. When Judas Maccabeus reconquered the Holy City, he ordered the temple to be cleaned of false images, and a new altar to be built, and the holy lamp to be filled with new oil. Everything had been defiled.

"And lo! Hidden away in a corner they found a small, sealed cruse of holy oil with just enough for one night. And the miracle happened. It burned for eight days. That one little flame kept the light in the temple till the new supply was found."

Her father's eyes, the rapture in his face and in his voice, as he launched forth on the symbolic meaning of the story.

"From the beginning of time, there have been wanderers who have strayed away from the fold, worshipping the false gods of the countries about them. But the few who keep God in their hearts keep the holy light burning."

That night, bathed in the poetry of ancestral memories, it seemed to her there was only one way to go on—to go back to her roots—back to the ghetto.

EPILOGUE

§ 1

Fanya opened her eyes, pushed back the covers of her bed, and watched, through her open window, sunrise spreading over the mountains. Her arms stretched over her head with the joy of breathing the clean air, sharp with the smell of spring.

Here in Oakdale, she was able, for the first time since childhood, to experience the dreamless sleep of complete oblivion throughout the night. Now she lay there, rested, unstirring, her whole being opened like a prayer to the silence of the sun-bathed hills, the fresh glow of morning.

Her attempt to go back to the ghetto had been blind and absurd. The glamorous memories of childhood, in which she had been caught up when she saw the old rabbi lighting the Chanukah candles, had faded with the light of morning. The dirt, the noise, the suffocating crowdedness of the tenements—she had outgrown them all. The old life of the ghetto was as much behind her as Henry Scott. No, there was no going back. But how to go on?—Where?

Anywhere, away from New York, away from everything she had known, she told Miss Hoffman.

The older woman listened sympathetically. After reflecting for a moment, she suggested:

"There's Oakdale—a heavenly village. Still and calm and rooted like a tree. The town boasts of the same families, the same number of people that lived in the village before the Revolutionary War." And then she added, "Having lived always in New York, you've never really seen America or met Americans. Oakdale is thoroughly American."

Half a day's train ride from New York, she found the quiet New England village of Oakdale. She came on a bleak March afternoon to look over the town, walking through unpaved streets of melting snow and mud. The little white houses, the plainly dressed people made up a world apart from the rest of the world. Even the dogs of Oakdale, instead of barking at her, as dogs bark at strangers, greeted her with friendly eyes and followed her about.

It was the mountains, mauve in the twilight, that decided her. The play of light and shade upon their heights filled their silence with an ever-changing pageant of color. Against those mountains, one could live alone and not be lonely.

Chance brought her to a small, unfurnished white house with green shutters, a short walk from the main street, which was for rent.

In April, she came to live in the green and white house, bringing her books and her typewriter. As she stepped off the train, a pale, slight woman, quaintly dressed, came toward her.

"I'm Mrs. Wilson, the doctor's wife," she introduced herself, leading the amazed Fanya to her automobile. "Miss Hoffman wrote us you were coming."

On the porch of her new house, neighbors waited to meet her and offer her welcome. When she opened the door, she saw the empty house miraculously furnished. A fire was burning in the wood-stove. Dotted swiss curtains on the window. A warm-colored rug on the floor. The room, with table, chairs, and a reading lamp, had the charm of things lived with and enjoyed. Each piece of furniture, mellowed with years, brought with it the old-fashioned atmosphere of the home from which it came. Even the bed in the bedroom was made up with fresh linen. And, spread out on the kitchen table, was a fresh, home-baked loaf of bread, a jar of homemade jam, fresh milk, a pat of butter, and a bowl of new-laid eggs.

She had come prepared to be alone. And there was this warm friendliness, this unexpected hospitality.

"Why, this is home!" Fanya cried. "It's so beautiful." She touched the oak table with appreciative fingers. "I thought such kindness was out of date."

"Perhaps it is in New York," the grey-haired woman who stood next to her said. "In the big cities, people are too worried, too unhappy to be kind."

Fanya studied the faces of her new friends.

"Are you people here happier than the people in New York?"

"I don't know about that," said the doctor's wife. "One thing is certain: we take more time to live." And then, she added, smiling, "You mustn't idealize us. You'll find out after you know us that we're only human after all."

"But this"—Fanya pointed to the loaded table in the kitchen—"this is being more than human to a stranger."

"You're not a stranger to us," said Miss Tracy, the young librarian. "We've read your books."

After the impersonal, apartment house life of New York, this learning to be a neighbor among neighbors, learning to take time to visit and time to have visits paid to her was like learning a new game. In New York, people were always watching the clock. Time was in a sieve, constantly running away from you. Here in Oakdale, time was infinite. She spent hours lying on her back, motionless, listening to the wind marching over the mountains, watching the clouds fly with the wind.

When the sun slowly melted the snow and ice from the mountains, and earth became warm and green and fragrant with a new sap of life, she planted a garden of vegetables and flowers. Waiting for the seed to take root and spring up from the ground, watching the earth resurrect itself from winter into spring was like being born again into a new harmony with the whole new-born world. Getting close to earth and sky and grass and trees quickened all her senses to the people around her.

Mrs. Chase, who lived in the house across the way, had been working in East Oakdale's chair factory during the past winter. Fanya talked to her in the warm evenings when they sat together outside on the porch.

"How is the work now?" she asked Mrs. Chase in sympathetic neighborliness when she returned, with tired steps, from work.

Mrs. Chase sat down, wearily, upon her porch swing.

"The women aren't so standoffish as they used to be," she confided. "They thought at first that I wouldn't talk to them."

"Why shouldn't you?"

"Well," she explained, with a tolerant smile, "people in East Oakdale aren't real natives. They're not in the same class as Oakdale proper."

There was a thoughtful silence.

"I tell you, family counts," she dug out from her broad experience. "Breeding is breeding. You can't make a silk purse out of a sow's ear."

So Oakdale turned up its nose at East Oakdale, because Oakdale dated its history from before revolutionary times and East Oakdale, a more recent settlement, was only about a hundred years old, composed largely of factory workers.

But even East Oakdale, which was not in the same class as Oakdale proper, had its social gradations. In East Oakdale, there was a sandy section, called "the island"—a dreary tract of sand and weeds on which stood dilapidated, tumble-down shanties, used mostly by a floating population of migratory farmhands. It was the unwashed slum section of Oakdale, this wretched ditch of weeds and sand, crowded with noisy children.

That the nice, carefully-brought-up children of Oakdale had to attend school with the children of "the island" was one of the disadvantages of the public school system, but after school hours, the mothers of Oakdale drew the line.

When Margery Chase brought two "island" girls home from school with her, Mrs. Chase lost her habitual patience.

"Don't dare bring those dirty brats into the house again," she warned her little daughter.

"Why not?" Margery insisted.

"You know quite well why not." Mrs. Chase was exasperated. "I've told you often enough."

Then, turning to Fanya, she explained, "It's not only the dirt I'm afraid of. It's their bringing up. The words they use."

"How is it that in a beautiful village like Oakdale there is this blot, this slum worse than the New York slums?" Fanya asked.

"Well," said Mrs. Chase, "I once read that wherever human beings live, one family out of every hundred goes downhill. And, of course, the people on 'the island' are the degenerate, downhill families of this section."

She pointed to a ragged old woman, riding slowly by in a one-horse buggy.

"See that awful looking creature! Fifty years ago, she belonged to the best families here. And look at her now! She's so dirty, she smells. They say she hasn't taken off her clothes for the last twenty years. I used to know when spring came," she laughed reminiscently, "because every spring time Jane put on her old straw hat. But now she's gone to seed like Rip Van Winkle."

Every day, at exactly nine o'clock, the old woman's buggy rattled past Fanya's house at the same slow pace. Her yellow-grey hair, thin and straggling, was always uncombed. The neglect and decay of years was in her solemn face. The eyes set deep inside her head seemed to see nothing before them. Joyless, griefless eyes, like dried out lakebeds of sand. Her muddy face had in it something shadowy and unutterably remote from the life around her. She wore a dirty sweater

worn into holes at the elbows, over a discolored spot-
ted gingham dress. Rubber boots covered her legs to
her knees.

The milk can which she carried to the station and
the stuffed bags which she carried from the station
seemed as empty and unsubstantial as the vacuous
stare of her eyes.

The events of her life were a worn-out story among
the neighbors. Her father had once owned a factory
that employed most of the workmen of the village.
Heavy losses in mining investments forced him to sell
the plant and go into farming.

Scarlet fever broke out on their farm. Her father,
then her mother died. Jane came out of it—totally deaf.
Somehow she could never get in touch with life again.
The decay of her farm and her person did not happen
all at once. At first she made an attempt to join the
village life. She even attended church on Sundays, but
her deafness shut her off from all that went on around
her. The final shock that severed her from human contact occurred when the man to whom she was engaged
left her to marry another girl.

Fanya ventured out to Jane's farm, in spite of the
neighbors' warnings. Her house was a moldering
wooden structure, overgrown with weeds and tall
grass. The front door and all the front windows were
shut. The ragged curtains, seen through the windows,
were black with dust. Decay and desolation spread
like a fungus growth over the place.

Looking for the old woman, Fanya walked around to
the back and found the kitchen door open. She glanced

in. What sickening disorder! The rank smell of mildew, grime, decay. The table loaded with dirty dishes, dirty pots, stale, leftover food, and rags. Over the unswept floor, old shoes, rusty tin cans, and rags were piled in untidy heaps. Jane, asleep, was sprawled out on the couch. Her loosened jaw revealed black, decaying stubs of teeth. Her muddy, inert face, with its shut eyes, was the face of a woman sunk in a stupor as insensate as death.

After that, she often walked by Jane's farm in order to watch her. She was milking the cows, one afternoon, as Fanya passed. Like the man who had lived so long among pigs that he took on the facial resemblance of a pig, this woman, deprived of human companionship, whose days were passed among her cows, seemed to have acquired the glazed eyes, the dulled demeanor of cows. As she milked, her fingers seemed to draw into her body something of the animals' calm.

The cows, the milk-pails, the barn were immaculate. Was it because she loved her cows so much that she lavished on them the cleanliness she failed to give her own person? Or was it because, in order to sell the milk to the city, her dairy had to maintain the required standard of cleanliness?

As she walked out of her barn with the full pails of milk, Fanya stopped her.

"Can you sell me a quart of milk?" she shouted at the top of her voice.

But Jane could not hear. Then Fanya wrote out her request.

The old woman's eyes opened wide at her.

"You want to buy milk from me?" Her voice had the hollow, metallic sound of the deaf.

"Yes," Fanya shouted back.

"Nobody here buys any milk from me."

A terrible patience was in the farmwoman's gaze.

What hurt could have made her so immune to hurt? Fanya wondered. After a pause, she asked:

"Well, where do you sell your milk then?"

"I ship it to the city dairy."

"Will you sell me one quart?"

Jane looked at her, still unbelieving. And then, seeing that Fanya meant what she said, she rinsed out a quart bottle and, after straining the milk in the separator, filled it and handed it to her.

Fanya gave her ten cents, the amount she paid to her milkman, but Jane gave her back five cents in change.

"That's all the city dairy pays me," she said. "That's all I'll charge you if you will come for the milk."

"Yes, I'll come." And, smitten with sudden pity for her, she added, "I'll get all my neighbors to come for milk, too."

The recluse shook her head unbelievingly.

"You must be a stranger in this town."

"Yes. I'm a stranger."

"Nobody but a stranger would want to buy milk from me."

The tranquil acceptance of her isolation lent a certain glamour to the ugly, old face—the glamour of those irrevocably removed from the touch of everyday people.

Fanya looked at her, wondering what to say, and Jane spoke again:

"Why did you come to this lonely town?"

"Do you think it's so lonely here? "

"If not for my cat and my cows—" she finished the sentence with a shrug.

Jane's excommunication roused Fanya from the idealized world her fancy had made of Oakdale. The ancient shadow that arrayed people against each other—the shadow of the old world—was right here among the Americans themselves. Clean people. Dirty people. The well-born and those not well-born. The few families who lived on inherited money politely aloof to those who had to earn the money they lived on.

She began a house-to-house campaign among the neighbors who had been so kind to her when she first arrived in Oakdale.

"There's one thing that can be done to reclaim Jane," she told them. "Draw her out of her isolation. Go to her and buy her milk."

"Buy milk of her? I guess not!"

Fanya's plea, that at first seemed absurd, later directed their suspicion to her.

"I wouldn't give a cat milk from her farm. They say she hasn't taken off her clothes in twenty years."

"She may be careless about her person, but she's clean about her barns and cows." She tried to reason with them.

"There's no excuse for dirt," maintained the immaculate Miss Tracy. "Soap and water are cheap. Anyone can be clean."

Even the minister's wife echoed the condemnation.

"Cleanliness is next to godliness," she declared. "Anyone who can suggest milk so dangerous to health—" and she looked at Fanya with eyes that placed her in the same anti-social ditch with Jane. "Besides," she added, "she brought everything on herself. We tried to get her back to church, but she slams the door in people's faces when they go near her."

"But people are not fixed objects like tables and chairs. The way in which you treat them and feel toward them is half of what they are to you."

Fanya paused in the midst of her defense to realize that the words she used were those Henry had used in her behalf.

Instead of winning them over, she had estranged them. The little social world of Oakdale grew mean and hard and airless.

In Jane's ostracism, Fanya saw her aunt thrusting her out of the house because her head was dirty, the disgust that the gentle Farnsworths must have felt at her letter, the fear that made Henry Scott flee from her uncivilized emotions.

Here, among the natives of this New England village, were exactly the same differences and struggles and smallness and bigness and kindness and cruelty as those she had known before in a world divided between people who had been in America a long time and those who hadn't. Something deeper, more far-reaching than the race barrier separated Jane from her nearest neighbors.

She was roused from her dark mood by the familiar trot-trot of Jane's buggy. She walked out to greet her.

The old woman stopped her horse and stepped down. She had an open newspaper in her hand.

"Look!" She smiled, and there was something like excitement in her usually hollow voice. "Here's someone from your New York."

Thrusting a newspaper into Fanya's hand, she pointed to the story of the proposed solo flight across the continent.

"Are you interested in aviation?" Fanya asked, bewildered by this enthusiasm.

"I'm interested in anything going on," the hermit said, with the calm enjoyment of those who view the world from an impersonal vantage point. "I read the newspaper every day."

Fanya was suddenly ashamed of her pity. Jane, the leper, towered over the impeccable little social world of Oakdale, free from the sordid comedy of personality in which the rest of the villagers were involved. Serene in her isolation as the mountains.

Jane shambled off to her cart, and Fanya saw how the villagers moved carefully aside as she passed them, unaware of their hygienic shudders.

Fanya looked after her until she disappeared. When she was gone, Fanya stood motionless at the door, holding the newspaper Jane had brought her, so strangely happy she was filled with smiling compassion for those who condemned her.

§ 2

Fanya had learned to be content to stand alone and look on at the village, and Jane's unexpected friendship warmed her from her hardly-won aloofness. Once again she expected things from life. But now things were coming to her. She was no longer seeking life.

Her hands went on mechanically with the ordinary, everyday routine, while she stood still—watching, waiting, expecting.

One evening, in this interlude of tranquility, the telephone rang. Miss Luke, the librarian from across the way, was on the wire.

"I've just sent a young man to see you," Miss Luke said. "I didn't know what else to do with him. I hope I'm not troubling you too much, but something must be done for him. He needs help and I thought—"

"But, Miss Luke," Fanya broke in eagerly, "it's no trouble! I'm glad you thought of me! If there's any-thing—Wait! Someone's knocking. Here he is, I know!"

A weather-beaten young man in a thick shabby sweater stood at the door. In awkward silence, he held out a note. His eyes, his face, with its grave, irregular beauty, were in such marked contrast to the poverty of his clothes that Fanya stared at him for a long moment before she read the note.

"Dear Fanya lvanowna," Miss Luke wrote, "The bearer of this letter, Vladimir Pavlowich, has just walked into the library and asked if I knew of any work. He seems deserving and when he said that he was half Russian, I thought of you and wondered if you, per-haps, would have any ideas about where he might get work. Won't you see if you can think of some opening—someone to whom we might send him. He is interested in books and reading—first editions, etc.—and he told

me he was an artist—but now is willing to do anything
that comes to hand—outdoors, indoors, anywhere. It is
a great problem, of course, and if nothing comes up,
I'll see if I can think of something. With thanks for any
attention you can give Mr. Pavlowich, and a hope that
you will know what to do.

"Hastily, always devotedly yours,
Elsie Luke."

Fanya looked up smiling from Miss Luke's somewhat bewildering note to meet the intent gaze of the
stranger's eyes. They were the steady, thoughtful eyes
of a man who had looked deep into life. They disturbed
and held her. She felt that she had never seen such
eyes before, and that she had always seen them.

"Tell me about yourself," she said, drawing up a
chair for him.

"I am looking for work," he said.

"I know.... But you look so competent, so able." She
glanced from his face to his strong sensitive hands.

"There are thousands of able young men looking for
work." He stared at the floor, and his body slumped
momentarily into the attitude of a poor man accustomed to being condemned for his poverty.

"Come, come, Mr. Pavlowich! You are not one of those
thousands." The mingling of pain and conviction in her
voice made him lift his eyes to hers and smile gratefully,
like a man who sees a friend in a room full of strangers.

"I'm a painter," he confided. "I've had to earn my
living as a commercial artist. I've spent years making
ads for soup and sausage and soap. But I got to the

point where I felt if I had to illustrate another sausage
ad, I'd blow up."

"And did you?" She laughed.

"Not exactly. I had enough saved up to keep me for
a year or two. I quit my job, thinking I'd go back to it
when my money gave out. But who could have fore-
seen these hard times? When I was ready to go back,
there was no job to go back to. I got so desperate that
I hired myself out as a bus boy in a sandwich shop,
and I wasn't even lucky enough to hold onto that job
for more than a day. The woman who hired me thought
I'd do, as long as I was willing, but the boss took one
look at me and fired me. He said he was sorry, but he
couldn't have a face like mine picking up dishes. After
that I took to the road. And here I am, willing to do
anything—I'll chop wood, I'll clean chimneys—"

She had an elbow on the arm of her chair where she
sat, her hand covering her mouth, and now she looked
up at him thoughtfully. "I knew at once that you were
an artist," she said.

"How did you know?"

"I don't know—I just *knew*."

She had taken the note from its envelope, and was
absently folding and unfolding it. Leaning forward, he
drew it from her fingers, and for an instant their hands
touched; and their eyes met, like long parted friends
who had suddenly stumbled upon each other.

She laughed then, very softly, and took the note back
and unfolded it again. Her eyes rested on his name.

"Vladimir Pavlowich," she announced, "how about
something to eat? I was just about to set the table when

you came in." The way in which she said his name gave
him welcome.

He followed her into the kitchen and watched her
beating some eggs.

"Here," Fanya said, in a warm, friendly voice, "you
cut the bread and toast it."

He began slicing the loaf, his eyes still upon her.

"See here, my friend," Fanya scolded, lifting up a
jagged slice, "you've got to do better than that."

He smiled down at her in a way that made her face
glow with youth and color. "I will do better," he said.

A few minutes later they sat down to table with
the easy familiarity of fellow-countrymen who dined
together all their lives.

"I knew that you were some kind of an artist the
moment I saw you," Fanya repeated as they finished
their coffee. "Or is it that we are both Jews?"

"No, I'm not a Jew," Pavlowich answered in a low
voice. "I'm a Russian Pole. But what does race matter
anyway? I mean here—now—between us—" He looked
at her in wonder.

"Oh, well, when a Gentile looks like a Jew there's
something terribly compelling about him," Fanya
said. Then suddenly self-conscious, she turned her
eyes away. "It's getting late. Hadn't we better find a
place for you to spend the night?"

Her embarrassment made her sound abrupt and
ungracious. For a moment he seemed to be about to
refuse. She almost saw "Don't bother" shaping itself
on his lips, and waited helplessly for him to say it.
She felt that if he did—if he turned and went away

alone—something more important than just this casual meeting would have gone out of her life.

But "Very well," he said—quietly, almost happily. And got up, and waited for her by the door.

*   *   *

They went down the road to Mrs. Brady, who kept an inn for tourists. At the path to the house, they paused. "Wait here a moment," Fanya said. "I'll see if there's room."

A plain-faced woman opened the door and led Fanya into a cheerful kitchen.

"Mrs. Brady," Fanya began, "there's a man out here who needs a room for the night. Can you take him in?"

"Yes, of course," Mrs. Brady replied. Her face brightened. "It's good of you to think of me. I'll give him the front room over the porch. Tell him to drive right in."

Fanya hesitated. "He—he hasn't any car, Mrs. Brady."

"Oh! He hasn't any car! How did he come? Where's he from?"

"Well, you see," Fanya explained, "he's just a homeless man out of work, who wants a place to sleep. I thought perhaps you—"

Mrs. Brady's kind eyes darkened with fear. "Oh!" she gasped. "Oh! It's too bad! I'm sorry. I—I couldn't take a man like that into my house."

"But Mrs. Brady," Fanya lowered her voice, "he's a nice man, really. I'll pay for the room. How much do you charge?"

"Oh, it isn't the money," the woman replied hastily.

"It's just that I don't like to take a stranger into my house."

"But don't you take in tourists?" Fanya asked.

"Yes—tourists. But this man from nowhere—he might be anything." A look of panic came into her face. "He might be a robber, or one of those gangsters that the papers are full of. I just couldn't. You understand, I'm sure. I wish there was something I could do, but I'm afraid of tramps."

One glance at Fanya's face as she returned to the road was enough to tell Pavlowich that she had been refused.

"Please," he said, "you're upset on account of me; and I don't mind in the least. Except that you are putting yourself to all this trouble. I ought to be ashamed of myself—I would be with most people. But you—you're different from other people, I guess." He stopped, like a man who has said too much. Then in a different, too matter-of-fact tone of voice—"As for being refused—well, you see, these hard-working farmers—the poorest of them have their cellars stored with supplies for the winter. A homeless man is out of their line."

This was too much for Fanya.

"You mean to say you defend them? Defend even their meanness, their narrowness?"

"How can you condemn them for something they are not even aware of? Now, for instance, on my way here to Oakdale, a constable started to arrest me—"

"Arrest you?"

"Don't you know there's a law in this state that any

man found walking on the highroad without money
can be locked up for vagrancy?"

His words brought a hot flush of anger to her cheeks.
"Is that how those who have protect themselves from
those who have not? Good God! What a terrible world
we live in."

"At any rate, it's a terribly interesting world. In fact
the constable who started to arrest me turned out to be
a good egg at that—according to his lights. In the first
place, he let me convince him that I wasn't a dangerous criminal; then he even took me to his house, gave
me the chance to clean his chimney and whitewash his
cellar, and paid me handsomely for it."

They walked on in silence. Fanya wondered at the
power she sensed in him—this power to look beyond
the thwartings and distortions of life that shut one person from another. She came to herself with a start and
realized that he was waiting for her to say what was to
be done next.

"Forgive me," she said. "I was thinking of what you
have just told me. Listen. This is what we'll do next.
We'll take you to one of the real people—one of the
native aristocrats of Oakdale."

He made a gesture of dissent.

"Oh yes, we will," she insisted. "Mrs. Brady was not
the person to have gone to. Everybody here goes for
everything to Miss Longworth. She is a kind of patron
saint of Oakdale. She has dozens of guest rooms where
she can put you up for the night."

"*Guest rooms!* No, please," he begged. "The last thing
I'd wish is to be of any trouble to you or anybody. It's

perfectly easy for me to sleep in some barn. It won't be the first time...."

"But you're not going to sleep out tonight. Come along. You'll see."

He laughed down at her, half in embarrassment, half in surrendered pride.

"What are you laughing at?"

"At nothing. Please don't misunderstand me. I was beginning to think I had forgotten how to laugh."

"I have no sense of humor," Fanya said. "Not now, at any rate. Now, I am going to get you a bed at Miss Longworth's. After that, maybe I'll laugh."

They went on together to the Longworth home.

It was a magnificent old house, situated on the corner opposite the church and lying well back in its own grounds. Only three persons and all those rooms, Fanya thought, as they walked up the granite terrace steps.

Again Pavlowich waited outside. As Fanya gave her name to the maid she caught a glimpse of a luxurious interior where Margery Longworth was playing cards with her father and mother, before an open fire. The sheltered security of this scene made her feel restless—it intensified the picture of the shelterless man out in the road. Wouldn't all this merely oppress him? Fanya thought, as she stood waiting. Why ask these people to do something? Couldn't she do something for him herself?

"Will you come in?" the maid said, and led the way.

Margery came forward with outstretched hand. "How do you do, Fanya lvanowna," she said, with her

ever-ready friendliness. "Won't you sit down?" Fanya
could never look at Margery Longworth's gentle,
puritan face without thinking that these quiet, thor-
oughbred features must be the reflection of a soul as
beautiful.

"I won't sit down, thank you," she said, nervously
crumpling her gloves in her fingers. "I am sorry to
break in on you at so late an hour. But I want to ask
you what to do. I'm trying to find a place for the night
for a homeless man. He's waiting outside."

"Yes?" Miss Longworth's voice rose slightly. "How
on earth did he come to such an out of the way village
as ours? Has he had anything to eat?"

"Oh, yes, he had his supper."

"Well, then, let me call up Mrs. Brady for you." And
she reached for the telephone.

"But I've been to Mrs. Brady, and she won't have
him."

"Perhaps she was afraid he couldn't pay for a room.
Let me fix it up."

"It wasn't a matter of money" —Fanya was surprised
to find that she had to keep exasperation out of her
voice— "I would have paid for him, but she was afraid
to take a stranger into her house."

A troubled look came into Margery Longworth's
face. "Well, that is so," she said sympathetically. "Mrs.
Brady lives alone, and you do hear of such terrible
things these days. Father made me promise not to pick
up any more hitch-hikers on the road."

She looked down in thoughtful silence for a
moment. "Let me see— Of course we must find a place

for him— Oh, I have an idea!" Her face lit up with the glad look that came into her eyes when she was being helpful to someone. "There's Doctor Wilson. He and his wife are so interested in problems of the unemployed."

She accompanied Fanya through the hall. "Good luck," she said, smiling warmly. As the door opened a chill wind blew into the warm house. "What a horrid night to be without a roof over your head." She shuddered. "I am so glad I thought of the doctor. Do call me up in the morning and tell me how he fixed him up."

Pavlowich saw Fanya's face as she came out of the shadows. "You've bothered enough," he said. "I want to thank you for all you've done. I'll be getting along now."

"Don't *you* let me down, too," Fanya said in a low voice.

"But I'll not have you bother anymore," he answered in the same tone.

"It's no bother. You must know that. Come. We're going to George Pomeroy. I'm only sorry I did not think of him before. He's the philosopher of the village. He's a carpenter by trade, but a born poet at heart. An old bachelor, and maybe a little crusty on the outside, as bachelors sometimes are, but he has the rarest, most stimulating mind when you get talking with him. He's a socialist and a communist and everything that's the poor against the rich. It isn't far—just around the corner at the foot of the hill." It was quite dark when Fanya and Pavlowich stopped at a gap in the fence on their left. A single light gleamed from a small window beyond a clump of bushes. "I'll just take a short cut through this path," she said. "It will save time. You wait here."

In response to Fanya's knock on the door of a small, somewhat dilapidated house there was a sharp bark from a dog inside. A moment later the door opened and a dog rushed out.

"Here! Wolf! Here!" a man's voice shouted. "Here! you blasted little fool! Come back here! Oh! Good-evening, Miss lvanowna! Come in! Don't be afraid of Wolf! He's like a lot of other people. He says a lot and never does anything."

Fanya laughed and was about to step inside, when the man called the dog again. "What's the matter with him?" he asked. "Here, Wolf! You noisy devil! Come back here!"

But Wolf failed to return.

"That's odd," he said. "I wonder what he's looking for?"

"I think I can tell you, Mr. Pomeroy," Fanya smiled. "He's looking for Mr. Pavlowich."

"Mr. Pavlowich? Who is Mr. Pavlowich?"

"He's a man I just left waiting over by the road. He's looking for a place to sleep tonight—"

"Why don't you take him to Margery Longworth? She's got rooms to burn. She's the person to see if you're trying to help out a tramp."

"But Mr. Pomeroy!" Fanya broke in hotly. "This man is not a tramp. He's just a homeless man out of work. I did go to Miss Longworth. And she passed the buck to Doctor Wilson. But now I know Doctor Wilson will only pass me on to someone else. I felt sure you'd take him in."

"Like hell I will! I have only one bed. I've got to get up tomorrow morning for a job. Thank God for that, these days. I don't keep open house for men of the road!"

Without a word, Fanya turned her back on him and walked out. She paused in the shadow of the shrubbery to watch the dog prancing around Pavlowich's feet, jumping up now and then to give him a friendly lick on the face.

"That dog has more humanity than the whole village," Fanya burst out.

She stooped to pat Wolf on the head. "You understand, don't you?" she said. "But go home, Wolf. Home!"

"Where are we going now?" Pavlowich asked, with a gallant acceptance of her wish to help him. Night after night he had had this same problem to cope with, and had come to accept it with a certain stoicism. Her sense of injury about something that had ceased to mean very much to him made him suddenly very happy.

"We're going back to my place," Fanya declared. "You've come to a thimble town." She laughed harshly. "These villagers are thimble-minded, and it's the nature of thimble minds to fear anyone they don't know."

"Thimble-minded?" he said. "That's an unjust word, a wrong word. Put yourself in their place. Think. With a century and a half of unchanging security back of them—with their age-old habit of seeing only familiar faces—and then, hearing of all the violence going on in the world—do you *really* blame them for hesitating to take a hobo into their homes? Do you?"

Fanya remained thoughtful for a moment; then she turned to him humbly. "No," she said slowly. "No, I don't. I was just falling back into the miserable old habit of scorning and hating and looking down on those who don't do as one thinks they should. It's a rare gift you have of being able to see other people's points of view, even when you are uncomfortably involved in them yourself. How much further you are along the road than I...."

He smiled down at her in silence.

They said no more to each other on the way home. Fanya was shaken with an excitement she had no means of recognizing for what it was. Pavlowich was walking more freely, his head up, drawing in great breaths of the night air, as though the night—for the first time in many days—had become a friendly thing. It was ten o'clock when they got back to Fanya's living room. It was a relief to be again in a small warm room after their cold, fruitless wandering. As they stood there, warming their hands at the low-burning log fire, Pavlowich noticed the empty wood-basket.

"Let me get you some wood," he said, eager for the chance to do something. In a moment he was out in the woodshed, the beat of his axe resounding through the house.

Fanya crossed over to the window where screened by the curtain she could watch him unobserved. The lantern nearby cast a ruddy light on his face, as his tall slim body swung back and forth to the rhythm of his axe. Every stroke of his strong arms vibrated through her feet, her spine, up through her whole body, flooding her with excitement.

She turned away from the window and looked about. His hat, his knapsack lying on the couch spread the aura of the owner about the room. She touched them gently with her fingers. They seemed to belong to the room—had always been there. The dust and rain of the road had infused into them a secret charm.

Her glance, striking the mirror, stopped; wonderingly, she examined herself. Her cheeks were flushed, her eyes full and wide with life. A chance encounter can do this to us; we meet somebody who responds to us; and before that response the dark muddle of our wasted years fades like night before sunrise.

Chance encounter? Her glowing, young face smiled at her from the mirror. For all its coincidence, something foreordained seemed to have brought them together. She had tried to push fate from her by taking him to those people, but here he was. He belonged here. Everything in her had stayed silent and grown ripe for this moment. Why, the very work he was doing rounded out the feeling of home. It seemed to her that she had never realized the comfort and the beauty of her house till she was seeing it through his eyes and sharing it with him.

Then he came in. And it is strange what may happen when the physical presence breaks in upon such a mood as hers. He was a stranger; he did not belong here by custom or by reason; and how could she ever tell him that he belonged by right? Coming in, glowing from his exercise, and boyishly proud of the basket of wood he put down, he had disturbed her in her most secret thoughts.

Suddenly she felt nothing but an intolerable strangeness, and if she could she would have shut a door between them, and locked it forever.

"I'll get the fire going in no time," he said.

Fanya forced herself to look at him. Like one bewitched, she traced his profile as he bent over the fender. The noble forehead, the strength stamped in the mouth and chin brought to her mind certain pictures of Rembrandt. And then she knew that the man *there* and the man she had been thinking of were one and the same person. And there was no longer any doubt or any fear.

When he glanced over his shoulder at her, she was sitting in her chair, looking quietly at him.

He finished tossing fresh logs into the fire, swept out the ashes, and took out a well-used laborer's handkerchief to wipe his hands.

"Perhaps you would like to wash up, now that your chores are done," Fanya said; and went and fetched him some clean towels.

He fingered them appreciatively. "It's a long time since I have enjoyed a luxury like this."

"Hot water?" Fanya filled a pitcher and brought it to him.

As he took the water, his hand fleetingly touched hers, and gave it a swift involuntary pressure that was as swiftly returned. Their eyes, meeting, fled in confusion, for indeed at that moment they had come upon one another in an unexpected place.

Fanya turned abruptly to the stove, and busied herself clearing up the pots and pans left from their supper. She brought a tray to the table with a steaming pot of tea, just as Pavlowich returned, washed and clean-shaven—the traces of the road gone from his face.

He looked about him, at the low bookshelf at the foot of the couch, the bright-colored flowers in their terracotta pots. "What a nice little place!"

"Yes, I like it, too. It's the first time in my life I have ever felt at home." And she told him how she had come a stranger to Oakdale, a year ago, of the reception she had met, how every article of furniture she possessed was a gift from these villagers. "That is why I could not let you go away. I wanted you, too, to find out that these cold New Englanders really have a heart. Once they know you, they'd share their last bite with you."

"Yes, I can believe that. I learned a lot about these folks from the constable who started to arrest me. I lived a week in his house and watched the farmers and their wives preparing to meet the hardships of winter. The men getting up in the early hours of the morning to chop down trees for their supply of fuel, the women toiling till late hours in the night canning and preserving. I used to despise them—parsimonious, provident—pinching and saving for a rainy day. But they make a noble passion of thrift. They wrest beauty from the dull routine of neatness and cleanliness. They're a heroic little people—these New Englanders."

*   *   *

"Heroic little people!" Fanya hugged the phrase to
her. It summed up her deepest feeling about these villagers. She sat quite still, breathing deeply....

He went on to tell her of his adventures on the road,
how he had learned to make a home of homelessness,
how much he had discovered in himself and others in
his rich experience of poverty.

"What does it matter, a meal more or less?" he said.
"Or whether the meal is roast duck or a can of beans?
It looked improbable that I'd have even a can of beans
tonight—and here I've been feasted—and not only
with food."

He broke off and lapsed into silence. The fire began
to go down; it grew quieter and quieter and still they
sat there, unstirring, unmoving. Without looking at
each other, they read each other's essences and flowed
together in understanding. Into each face had come
that look of release—exiles in strange lands, suddenly
granted a vision of home.

The shrill whistle of the midnight train roused them
from this trance of silence.

"Well, I must go and let you sleep," he said, reaching for his hat.

"No," she said. "No." She paused a moment and
then, "I'll tell you," she went on, "I have only one bed,
but we can fix up a place for you on the floor in the
other room. You'll find some quilts in the pine chest
there. Fix yourself up as best you can."

"Oh, but I can't impose on you like that. I—I'd like
to, but I can't."

"It is too late for you to go elsewhere. Besides—I want you to stay. If only you'll be comfortable enough."

"It's not a matter of comfort. It's you I'm thinking of. This is a small town, and they've been so good to you, and you want to live here."

"If I'm not afraid, why should you be?"

"But I am afraid."

There was such clear honesty in his look that she evaded his eyes. She began agitatedly to straighten magazines on the table. Feeling his gaze still fixed piercingly upon her, she started and gave her head a little shake.

"Nonsense! What is there to be afraid of?" She said it as lightly as she could, but her voice sounded strange in her ears.

He was silent for a long time. His eyes, which had been directed outward upon Fanya, turned inward and darkened.

"Well...then..."

He picked up his knapsack and moved toward the outer room.

"Good-night," she said, closing the door after him.

"Good-night."

She undressed quickly, and lay very still under the covers, hearing his every move in the other room. Now he dropped his shoes on the floor. His hands fumbled at the buckle of his jacket. She heard the careful putting down of his watch on the chair.

He walked to the window and lifted the sash. The light of the candle must have wavered as the wind blew in. His firm step crossed over to the mantle where the candle burned. Then darkness. For a while everything was still, then the stillness was broken by his restless turning from side to side. She lay tensely quiet, seeing every feature of his face rising out of the darkness before her. ("He was a man of sorrows and acquainted with grief.") Her fingers longed to feel the shadowy lines of his eyes and the deep grooves of his forehead. Every line of his weather-beaten face had meaning within meaning for her.

In the darkness she became aware of her hands lying so still there on the covers. Those hungry hands that reached so greedily for life that was forever escaping them—those hands lay still. A tremendous stillness, a tremendous peace held her excitement in an ocean of quiet. All she had ever longed to be, had been secretly, silently growing and ripening in her breast. All she had searched for so fiercely all her life had come unsought to her own door—within her own heart.